# BAPTIZING THE DEAD AND OTHER JOBS

# MICHAEL WILLIAM PALMER

# BAPTIZING THE DEAD
## AND OTHER JOBS

BAUHAN PUBLISHING
PETERBOROUGH, NEW HAMPSHIRE
2019

Library of Congress Cataloging-in-Publication Data

Names: Palmer, Michael William, author.
Title: Baptizing the dead and other jobs : essays / Michael William Palmer.
Description: Peterborough, New Hampshire : Bauhan Publishing, 2019.
Identifiers: LCCN 2019030062 (print) | LCCN 2019030063 (ebook) |
 ISBN 9780872333024 (trade paperback) | ISBN 9780872333031 (epub)
Classification: LCC PS3616.A3436 A6 2019  (print) | LCC PS3616.A3436 (ebook)
| DDC 814/.6--dc23
LC record available at https://lccn.loc.gov/2019030062
LC ebook record available at https://lccn.loc.gov/2019030063

Book design by Kirsty Anderson
Text set in Jan Tschichold's Sabon, with Acumin Pro headers
Cover Design by Thao Thai

BAUHAN
PUBLISHING LLC
PO BOX 117  PETERBOROUGH NEW HAMPSHIRE 03458
603-567-4430
WWW.BAUHANPUBLISHING.COM
Follow us on Facebook and Twitter – @bauhanpub

MANUFACTURED IN THE UNITED STATES OF AMERICA

# Contents

# 7-Eleven Clerk

For the first week and a half after Blake, Jen, Ariel, and Scott drowned in a dark cave on Y mountain, I spent most of my time staggering around my apartment like a wounded criminal, lying down in the dry bathtub, and going outside only to visit the sealed-over cave or to attend a funeral. I hadn't gone to work once, nor given an explanation for my absence beyond "personal reasons," so I was surprised when I went back for my paycheck to find out I still had a job if I wanted it.

I was working the graveyard shift at a low-activity 7-Eleven not far from Utah Lake, and that was where I had been the night Blake died. Because of that, plus the actual shudder I felt in my spine at the thought of refilling the nacho dispenser or pretending to clean the grill, I did not want to go back there. But I had rent to pay and was out of gin and groceries, so I re-took the job. The shift was from 11:00 p.m. to 7:00 a.m., and nothing really happened after beer sales stopped. Officially, that time was 1:00 a.m., but it was almost 1:00 now, and I knew better than to look out the glass windows to the empty pavement thinking I was finished for the night. Most shifts, someone would run in late, trying to beat the clock.

At 1:20 a guy pulled up in a Jeep Cherokee and left it running while he pushed through the front doors as though they opened to an emergency room. He hauled two 24-packs of Keystone Light to the front and slammed them on the counter. He wiped his brow.

"Sorry, I can't sell it after 1:00," I said.

"Come on man, there are like fifty girls at my house right now." The top two buttons of his shirt were unbuttoned. I honestly didn't know if there was a red flag in the system if I made an alcohol sale after 1:00, but I wasn't going to figure it out for him.

"Sorry, can't do it."

For a moment, his eyes filled with mischief, as if he might take the beer and run. Maybe he remembered how heavy the cases were and thought better of it. He tried again to argue with me, but I was already listening to the low, *Dawn of the Dead* hum of the store and thinking about how I would spend the next five-and-half hours.

After he left, I walked into the back area where the drinks were stocked and drank a stolen beer of my own. Then I walked behind the register and sat down, positioning myself in front of the cigarettes so it would look to the surveillance camera like I was organizing them. I was pretty sure the manager didn't have time to view the surveillance tape to check up on me, but I wanted to be in the position of doing something in case he did happen to fast-forward through it.

~

This was their route: winding in Blake's mom's Jeep above Seven Peaks Waterpark, parking in an unfinished residential area, exiting into the night and climbing the steep but familiar hill until it veered off into a mysterious cement oasis, half a mile up the mountain. Some of the dirt on that hill was loose and you had to grab at the sagebrush and dry trees for balance. In my head, and on the back of my nightly to-do list, I traced those directions, pictured the dark water shining where the moon hit. I could see their bodies slowly submerging until their heads were cutting through the glassy water like dorsal fins.

There was an underwater tunnel that connected the first cavern to the second, with a rope affixed to both sides to guide a person through. On the other side, there was just enough vertical space for one's head and shoulders and a little more. The second cavern had room for five or six people.

I'd been in that water once before, but never the second cavern. It was possible to stay in the first part—just wade in the chest-high water for a while and get out. But the point was to go under and re-emerge on the other side.

I didn't consciously worry that anyone would drown there, but I was still afraid. The night I went there was very quiet. The water was very still and, when I shone my flashlight on its surface, I had a hard time determining that it was, in fact, water and not just darkness. I hesitated before stepping in, staring at the effect of my flashlight

8

beam sinking in the dark water. I stripped down to my boxers and touched the water with my feet. My skin tightened and my veins started to change color.

I obsessed over that cavern so often afterward that I can picture it clearly, as if I had seen it all. But the fact is, I had been too afraid to swim through.

Blake told me that it was as good as anything he'd felt to rise, dripping, onto the weeds and dirt. The mountain air warm and bright.

∼

Blake had a lot of tattoos. I liked the railroad spike tattoos on his shins the best. He also had two half sleeves, the one on his left arm more colorful. I never paid a lot of attention to the individual parts of that tattoo, but as a whole I knew it looked like a waterfall flowing down onto a pink lotus flower above his elbow. Besides the water and the flower, all I could remember of Blake's sleeve was the color: red lines following the curves of the water, dark green blurring into black on the outside.

Blake donated his organs when he died, and I liked the idea that someone might be walking around with his tattooed skin. Blake once told me that one of the things he liked best about tattoos was the way they mapped a person's life—for him, there was nothing sad about a straight edge tattoo on someone smoking a cigarette, or the name of a long-irrelevant lover scrawled across someone's heart, because of the way those tattoos were honest about the past. He liked all of that, and I loved the vision of someone walking down the street, a second-hand lotus flower shining from his arm.

∼

At 3:30, two intoxicated young women wearing cowboy hats walked into 7-Eleven. They both had long blonde hair that fell from under their hats and down their shoulders. I thought at first that they might be sisters, but their faces were too different. They asked me what it was like to work there, and asked if I saw some crazy shit. I told them that that night I had seen a tired, middle-aged guy and a sad teenager, both of whom bought Doritos. They said that sounded boring; one of them showed me her "country dance"—a boot-slapping *Riverdance* and square dance blend—without my asking. I didn't have a lot of response to that. They bought some beef jerky and energy drinks and left.

Even though the coffee at Sev starts to taste like seething hatred after three cups, it still had the intended effect of keeping me awake, shaky and irritable through my shift, so I poured another cup and walked around the store, waiting for it to get lighter outside.

~

When Blake's mother Laura went to the morgue to identify his body, the morgue workers accidentally brought out the wrong body first. They brought out Scott, whom Laura had never met. When they pulled back the sheet, she was relieved. This was not Blake; Blake had not drowned. There had been a mistake. Quickly the workers realized their error, covered Scott's face, and wheeled out Blake for proper identification.

Laura said Blake looked like he was still trying to breathe. She threw herself onto the body and tried to force CPR. It took four men to pull her off. When they did, her mouth was dripping blood like a vampire, her eyes just as red.

~

I had about half an hour to go in my shift, so I started tying up the trash bags and carrying them out to the dumpster where a group of magpies were gathered as if they were expecting me. It was warm, and it looked like the purple, pre-dawn light had been spilled over everything from the green dumpster to the lake in the distance. The magpies especially looked shiny and full of energy covered in that kind of lighting. I looked forward to seeing them in the mornings because of that, and because they had attitude. They watched me as though scrutinizing my ability to throw the bags in the dumpster, only begrudgingly and at the last second moving out of my way. The outside traffic was switching on—I heard cars starting and doors closing. Streetlights were still shining, but the sun was close. My body was tired but sensed that my shift was almost over. After work I took the bus home. My girlfriend Anna was asleep and would be starting her day soon. I mechanically went through toothbrushing motions and fell asleep next to her smelling of coffee, my mind full of color.

～

That morning, I dreamt about the deserts in Snow Canyon. It wasn't the first time and I wondered why I kept having those dreams. It wasn't the deserts that ran through my mind every time I fell asleep, but an obsessive imagining of Blake's last thrust for air, his last thought before he drowned.

The dreams had few outstanding features. They were fragmented blurs of brightness with the occasional recognition of a memorable landscape scar. I would be lying on a large, red rock with two overwhelming blues coalescing overheard—the blue color of desert heat sticking onto the blue sky like a contact lens. I didn't feel the inconveniences of sweat or coarse sand on my skin, only the warm buzz of insignificance. Sometimes a lizard would skitter across a rock. Mostly, though, the dreams were just colors stirred together—quiet and bright.

～

Blake donated his eyes, too. They were coffee-black and seemed to see more intensity in things than I ever did. I wondered if any of that would carry over to the new owner. I wondered if I would recognize the eyes if I saw them again.

～

I woke up around 2:00 p.m. Anna was gone to work. I spent the afternoon looking at our mediocre view until birds in the driveway started to chirp loudly. I made coffee and started thinking about Blake's lotus flower. Up until that time I had never cared about a flower that didn't eat insects or grow on a cactus, but the lotus reminded me of Blake. First, because of the tattoo; also because when he and his mom lived in Orem, they had had a pink glass lotus flower in their front window that I used as a landmark to locate his house, which I otherwise would have had trouble distinguishing from its neighbors.

I took volume *L* of the maroon encyclopedia from 1975 off my shelf and brought it into the dry bathtub with me. The encyclopedia said that lotus flowers grow in water—their roots are planted in the soil of a pond or river bottom, while the leaves float on top of the surface. The leaves are brightly colored. The brightness of the flower combined with its aquatic life seemed radically unlike the Utah County landscape we'd both grown up in, all dryness and mountain peak. I was interested that where I would likely have a tattoo of a poplar or a cliff, Blake—every bit the Utahn I was minus a one-year stint in Vegas and another in Denver—went for the lotus flower. I wondered if the tattoo had something to do with Blake's Hare Krishna days. We grew up in the same area, but he was one of the only people I knew who grew up there without ever being Mormon.

I got out of the bathtub and called Blake's mom. I called every few days, supposedly to see how she was doing, but mostly because I wanted to hear her voice, to talk to someone whose mourning ran all the way through her bloodstream, hair, and bones. Someone who wanted none of the grief-assuaging, customer-service tones of comforters. As the phone rang, I thought I would ask what she knew about the lotus flower, symbolically or otherwise, but thought better of it when I heard her slow voice on the phone.

"Hi, Laura, it's Michael."

"Oh, hi, Michael."

I didn't want to ask how she was, either, so I asked if there was anything I could do for her. I knew the unlikelihood of that, but I wanted to see her and had nothing else to do. She said she would like it if I would come by and go through Blake's old things before she donated what she didn't want.

"Also," she said, "there have been a lot of flies in the house lately." Laura lived in Hobble Creek Canyon, miles east of Springville. Insects were always a problem; every year she hired someone to apply a sticky chemical around the perimeter of the house and in all of the crevices to keep them out. But apparently the flies were fighting through that chemical and dying on the other side, especially in Blake's room. I told her I could come over right now and she said that would be nice.

I sped along I-15 to the second Springville exit and wound up the canyon to Laura's house. I was used to the drive; Blake had lived there off and on, and I had driven him home plenty of times. I rolled down my window and breathed the juniper scent of canyon air.

The house was behind a golf course, distinguished from the other cabins by its red roof. There was nowhere to park in the driveway where Laura's car was, so I parked on a flat area of leaves and twigs that looked like it used to be a campground.

I knocked on the door and waited. When Blake and I came here late at night, we had snuck in to avoid waking Laura up. Usually we ducked in to get something and then left again, so the house stayed dark and limited in my mind. I didn't see the whole place until I was asked to housesit and feed Darwin and Marx, their cat and dog. I spent the night there, sleeping upstairs in a room looking out over the neighbor's dog pen below and through the trees and the golf course in the distance. I made coffee in the morning, and listened to the rain fall on the red roof at night, making the sound of anxious fingernails tapping against a wooden desk.

The house was quiet; Laura had a fire going in the fireplace and some papers spread out on her table. Before she showed me Blake's room, she warned me again about the flies, reminded me that I didn't have to deal with the problem. She could do it herself or hire someone to do it. I asked her to show me. She opened the door. She hadn't done much to change the room—there were dirty shirts on the bed, books and records on the floor. The dead flies were all over the windowsill, overflowing onto Blake's bed below and covering the bed's surface well past the pillow. They coated parts of the floor, sometimes two or three flies deep. I said I would vacuum them. Laura said thanks and said I was welcome to anything I wanted of Blake's. Then she walked into the kitchen.

I waded through the room, feeling ambivalent about looking through Blake's things without his having a chance to arrange or explain them. Miniature model trains that he had sent to artists around the country to paint and return sat on shelves along the perimeter of his room. Other than that, it was mostly dirty laundry and old notebooks on the bed and floor. There were shelves of books and boxes of CDs in the corners.

The flies vacuumed up pretty easily but I was stupefied by how many there were. Their bodies overflowed from the windowsill into open drawers and onto the carpet below. They weren't blanketing the entire floor, but I found them everywhere—in the closet, under the bed, inside Blake's shoes.

～

When Laura saw his body for the last time in the crematorium, all of Blake's reusable parts had been removed. He looked like a collapsed bunker, a shell on a rolling steel table under clinical lighting. When Laura told me this story, I pictured a stack of organs lying next to Blake's hollowed out body, and for some reason it wasn't a disturbing image, as if some part of Blake would live on as long as those organs were functioning.

The workers paused there for a minute and let Laura get a last look. She stopped them when they tried to move the body into the furnace. She kept doing that for a while, then she let everyone go.

The workers inserted the body, hit a red button, and the burning began. After a while they hit another button and the burning stopped. Then they hit a button and let the furnace burn a little longer, to be sure.

～

I found Laura in the kitchen and she asked me if I was all right. I said yes without thinking. Darwin jumped on the table and I stroked his back. I decided this was as good a time as any to ask if she knew, specifically, where pieces of Blake had gone.

Laura drank her coffee and said, "I'm not sure about that." Another sip. "This is what I have left of him." She walked to the cupboard and pulled out a ceramic container that looked like it might have held sugar. She opened it up and I saw Blake's ashes inside. The correct term is cremains, I guess, but what was inside that jar looked exactly like the ashes of a fire that had burned hard for a long time. The bigger pieces of bone looked like small rocks that had turned white in the heat but had not burned.

"How much were they able to reuse?"

"Well, I know they can't use tattooed skin," she said. Then she

14

scooped some of Blake's ashes into a plastic Ziploc bag for me. She told me that Blake's tattoo artist said he could mix the ashes into ink and give her a tattoo with it if she wanted. She was going to get a railroad spike on her ankle next week.

$\sim$

I was disappointed to learn that Blake's tattooed skin wasn't reusable, but I could still imagine someone walking around in the world, seeing through Blake's eyes. I pictured her in my head: she was five-foot-seven with long black hair and wore a red Stanford sweatshirt even though she never went to Stanford and never would go there. She grew up in a small town and during the summer at night she drove to 7-Eleven at 2:00 a.m. to buy the Limited Time Only Slurpee. Sometimes she drove back home, sometimes on to the nearest lake. She knew the difference between jumping into a lake and a pool. I saw her look into the water, unconcerned with depth or temperature because, at night in the summer, the whole world was a large, cool lake. She kept her poise as she walked into the water, one foot at a time, careful, delicacy in each step. Then she dove outward, face first, with a swish, kicking her way down through the water. She fell away from the surface for a while, then came back to it and dove again. Anyone with those eyes would know how good it is to dive underground and let the water swallow you. And how good it feels to come back.

I saw her dive into the water and return to the surface; dive under and return again. Then I walked back into Blake's room to finish vacuuming the flies.

# Lawn Mower

By any math, later summers are worse, but the hottest summer in my memory is the one before I started 9th Grade. The mountains seemed to be on fire throughout July—one fireworks accident after another. We usually ate our dinners outside in the summer, and when the wind blew, the smell of smoke covered the violet scent of my mother's lilacs. My friend Brad and I would climb onto his roof to watch the fires. His roof sloped east toward Mount Timpanogos, and the shingles were white, which kept them from burning us too badly. We sat on towels and used binoculars to look for smoke. We could also see construction equipment on the other side of the orchard. Neat rows of apple trees divided our neighborhood from Locust Avenue on the other side. Those trees were about to go down, too, to make way for apartment buildings and houses big enough to bury ours in shadow. We watched a helicopter dump water on the mountain, and then head back toward Utah Lake to refill. It seemed to be just the one helicopter responsible for the whole mountain—a low-rank insect performing an endless task.

Along with watching *The Simpsons*, caffeinated drinks, or staying up after 9:00 p.m., climbing onto the roof was one of the many things allowed at Brad's house but forbidden at my own. Or rather, no one was there to stop us. His mom had died the previous winter, his dad worked a lot, and his sisters were grown and had moved out.

This was also the summer Brad claimed to have a girlfriend— "Kristina with a *K*." Even at the time, I suspected she was made up, although he invited me to smell his fingers if I didn't believe him. But whether his relationship status had truly changed or not, his way of talking had: Brad seemed to know things not only about girls, but about death, and cars, and shoplifting, and what life would be like for us as teenagers. I usually nodded along with what he was saying as if I understood, too astounded by what he knew to even correct him on his swearing or crassness. All those years trying to get him to go to church, I felt genuine pain that he was refusing something vital by declining. Now, for the first time, I wondered what knowledge he was gaining in his churchless delinquency that I was missing.

~

My mom paid twenty dollars a week to get the lawn mowed. We lived on a half-acre lot and my brother and I split the lawn and the payment. The previous summer, whenever I had cash, Brad and I would ride our bikes to the card shop on Main Street and I'd spend my money on basketball cards. If I had money left over, I'd buy a soda at Harts and drink it on the way home. Then Brad and I would compare our card collections on his trampoline. But this summer, he was trying to convince me to buy his cards instead. He said he wanted to save up because Kristina "expected certain things." When I asked him what he meant, he chuckled and shook his head. When I said he didn't know what he meant himself, he said, "You'll see."

~

Sometime in August, my family went to Utah Lake with the Beagleys, who had a boat. I loved to be pulled on the tire-shaped tube behind it. I held on tight to the handles, leaned with the turns, and felt I couldn't be shaken. I made a point of bragging about it, and on the next run Brother Beagley jerked the wheel hard, a wave rocked my spine, and I let go and toppled into the water.

After some good-natured taunting, I stayed ashore for the next run and pouted.

I walked up and down the dock for about five minutes before getting bored, and then decided to walk around the lake. I remember the sun lighting up the water as bright as metal, and seeing insects swarming a dead carp. By the time I felt the sting of the sun on my neck, I'd lost sight of the boat. My family had lost track of me, too, and by the time we found each other, it felt as though the sun's rays had burrowed under my skin.

I thought I'd covered myself in spray-on sunscreen, and had promised my mom as much, but once the burn set in, it looked as though I had used a white marker to scribble on my pink body. The pain was immediately sharp enough to require all of my focus, and over the next few days, the burn transcended physical pain, turning first into illness, and then into a feeling I would remember once I experienced real, all-consuming grief years later: every move I made brought me to the verge of tears. The Vitamin E balm meant to soothe my skin felt like it ripped an icy wound anew.

I became a basement Gollum creature after that. When Brad came over to invite me to his roof, I nearly vomited at the prospect of going outside. I spent the last days of summer lying as still as possible on top of my sheets. After a few days, I started to carefully peel away sheets of skin from my shoulders. It resembled dried glue. In that way, the sunburn gave me a reptilian rite of passage into adolescence. I'd shed my skin, but while I might have walked outside afterward feeling like a new person, what I remember when I think about it now is what I left behind.

# Dialer

Every Mormon family has its cautionary tale. Ours was my cousin Joe, who renounced the church, started doing drugs, and eventually moved from Utah to Portland. I was only a kid when Joe started his slide, but I knew all about him. He always wore black to family reunions, embracing his role.

When I was fifteen, I told my mom that I didn't want to go to church anymore, and Joe came up right away. She told me it was okay that I was questioning my beliefs—the church emphasized strong personal testimonies, and you didn't get one without some work. I was certainly free to keep my mind open, but I should remember that not going to church was the wire that had tripped Joe into a downward spiral. First, Joe said he didn't want to go to church, then he started swearing, then drinking, then drugs, and "who knows what else in Portland."

"One day he's a popular kid who plays sports, the next day he's a sullen layabout smoking drugs in the garage," she said.

I was offended by her bringing up Joe's tale, especially because I had announced myself to be straight edge for life. "Just because I'm not sitting in church for three hours every week doesn't mean I'm going to throw my morals out the window," I said, but the way she described it is pretty much exactly what happened—it just took a few years. By my nineteenth birthday, I had lost my scholarship and dropped out of college. Straight edge was a memory. I was working at a call center, and spending my scant paychecks on toy robots and pot to smoke in the garage.

~

The call center was called Western Wats, and my job title was "Dialer." It was the second job I'd ever had. My first had been at a fast food restaurant called Arctic Circle (slogan: "Get the good stuff"), and I'd been fired after two months because I wasn't making enough progress. People hired at the same time I was had already learned to work the register, while I was still handing out precarious and misshapen ice cream cones to unhappy customers. Even so, the firing blindsided me, and the self-doubt I'd incurred as a result led me to believe I was permanently unemployable. When I got the job at Western Wats—with an assist from my friend Crystal, who already worked there—I barnacled onto it. My grateful attitude instantly propelled me into the upper echelon of dialers, and my status with the company improved even more when, unlike everyone else who had been hired with me, I didn't quit or vanish after two months. The job paid $7.10 an hour and consisted of calling strangers from a beige cubicle and asking them to provide feedback on the quality of their experience at a car dealership, or to rate the customer service of their phone company on a variety of criteria, using a scale from 1 to 10. Almost no one lasted there, and the few who did worked only fifteen to twenty hours a week.

I worked thirty to thirty-five hours a week: afternoon shifts on Monday through Thursday and the full shift on both Saturday and Sunday. After a few months of this, I internalized the call center protocol of relentless inquisitiveness delivered with absolute neutrality. Besides convincing someone to take the survey, Western Wats trained us to do essentially three things: speak with a gung-ho tone ("They can hear when you're smiling—and when you're not"), give non-committal responses such as "I see" and "I understand" so as not to influence future answers, and ask "effective, probing follow-ups" on the open-ended questions. "What else?" is an example of an effective probe; "Anything else?" is not. (The former makes the interviewee feel as though she's required to give a follow-up, whereas the latter suggests we can move on if she just says no.) The basic goal of any call was to get someone through a fifteen-minute survey without conveying anything whatsoever beyond the cheerily-delivered script.

There is something vampiric about this mode of conversing—taking in as much information as possible while giving nothing of yourself. Even so, the call center tactics made me, if not a better, at least a more durable conversationalist than I'd ever been. In the past, I felt out of place in nearly any conversational setting. But after working as a dialer, if I didn't have an interesting or clever response ready to go, I knew I could always fall back on probing questions. Just as in the surveys, people will often say a lot if you don't give them the option not to.

One day my mom, doing her best to contain her frustration with the church-free and directionless adult I'd become, asked me, "What is it you *want*, exactly?"

"I just want to live my own life," I said.

She rolled her eyes. "What *else?*" she said, using my own question against me. I said, "That's it," but I ground her question in my teeth the whole bus ride home. I couldn't come up with a satisfactory answer, and lurched back into platitudes instead. *Good things come to those who wait; John Stockton sat on the bench for two years before starting.*

~

I lived in a tiny basement apartment in Orem, Utah, with one roommate. The place was enough of a shithole that even my rosy, at-least-it's-not-my-parents'-basement vision wouldn't allow me to spin it as anything else. It had stained, gray carpet, and the "walls" that made up our two "bedrooms" were flimsy beige dividers, similar to the cubicle dividers at Western Wats. We shared a bathroom. It looked like there had once been a medicine cabinet in there, but it had been ripped from the wall. What remained there was a loosely secured sink and an old bathtub with a showerhead designed for hobbits. The place smelled as if it had just rained Febreze.

The upstairs of the house was rented by a group of four guys in a Christian ("NOT Mormon") metal band called Adjacent to the Lord. They practiced in the garage, and when they would play the cereal bowls on our coffee table would shake and vibrate, Godzilla-style.

My roommate was a transgendered woman named Sharon. We'd grown up together, and when we first signed the lease, she still publicly identified as a man and went by Kyle.

One night, drinking coffee at the Village Inn up the street, just as the caffeine fidgeting started and I thought we were ready to leave a tip and walk back home, she asked me if I'd ever heard of gender dysphoria.

My answer was no, but since the question wasn't about our usual topics of girls, possible road trips, or rankings of movies, I didn't even say that. Sensing something was coming, I just looked at my speckled mug half-full of coffee. In the 2:00 a.m. diner light, the coffee looked like grease. I stirred, as if that was a response.

"Well, basically it's the feeling that you were born in the wrong body, if that makes sense," she said.

"I see."

"Anyway . . . this will probably be weird. And if you aren't cool with it, that's fine, I understand, and I'll move out. But I think you should know I feel like that. And I think I'm ready to change. I'm going to. Starting with my name."

We didn't say anything for a while, until I asked, "What else will you change?"

"Well, lots of things. Everything."

"I see."

~

Later, Sharon told me she was certain I was "freaked" when she told me, but the feeling I recall is surprise. When falling asleep that night, I remember thinking hastily that there must be aspects of every person I knew nothing about. Then my thoughts shifted to what this meant for me. I fell asleep hoping that in her gender transformation, Sharon would stop being such a slob and do the dishes once in a while. I had two sisters and knew that girls being cleaner than boys was a stereotype, but I was hoping it was a stereotype Sharon would embrace.

~

Besides changing her name, Sharon had already gone shopping for new clothes, knew which hormones to start taking, the price of eventual surgery, and was in e-mail contact with members of trans communities in several big cities nationwide. She wore long skirts and carried a handbag. She had a purple and black tattoo of her own design inked on her lower back; it was a rectangular shape that reminded me of a magic carpet. Sharon said it symbolized "wholeness." She had a long, thin body, but she was self-conscious about her hands and jawline.

Unfortunately, so strongly did she exert herself in her transition that she had no work ethic left over to channel into maintaining baseline standards of apartment cleanliness. Post-transition, she was twice the slob she used to be, which was three times the slob I was. I didn't wipe down the floorboards daily, but I didn't consider a pile of dirty laundry to be a pillow, either.

Besides transitioning, Sharon had only one other goal: move to New York. She saw the apartment, and its extremely low rent—which cost less than what we paid for pot—as a means to an end. As for me, I was just taking the easiest, cheapest path available, without caring where it led.

At first, I didn't take her desire to move to New York too seriously because it was a story I'd heard a thousand times. It seemed like everyone in Utah County with a tattoo sought refuge in either Portland, as Joe had done, or New York City. But only the ones with rich parents actually made it, and only for as long as they could convince their parents to keep sending them money. I ran into them on the bus sometimes, recently returned, lugging around a chest of gripes about how, when they lived in New York, everything didn't shut down on Sunday, the people were much more open-minded, and there was more going on in one square block of Manhattan on a Monday night than in all of Utah County's history. They would often end their remarks by saying, "You can't understand how different it is unless you've lived there," as if I had been begging them to make it clear to me.

But in Sharon's case, I couldn't really object. I rolled my eyes when she said, "There's nowhere for me to just *be*, you know?" but she had a point. It took a certain amount of courage for her just to go grocery shopping, where stares and whispers were almost guaranteed, and she felt a ubiquitous threat of something worse.

So she was motivated. And she kept working hard—also at a call center, but a different, better-paying one called Convergys—overtime and weekends, whatever she could get. She cut back on the pot, saved enough for a plane ticket and two months' rent, and arranged an apartment in Brooklyn with Dresden, a girl she met online. Before I knew it, I was giving her a hug at the airport. She told me I was welcome to join her out there—"leave behind this repressive hole of misery," in her words—but I had thirty-six dollars in my bank account and, at that time, I was still enrolled in school. I just laughed off the suggestion and told her maybe I'd come visit sometime.

~

A few months later, though, things changed. I lost my scholarship, and without it I couldn't afford to stay in school, so my life was pretty much limited to working at Wats and getting wasted on the balcony, sometimes with Adjacent to the Lord, sometimes by myself.

One such night, I called Sharon. It was past midnight on the East Coast, but she answered.

"How would you rate your overall experience in New York, on a scale of 1 to 10, where 10 means entirely satisfied and 1 means entirely dissatisfied?" I asked.

"20," she said.

"Using a scale from 1 to 10, please."

"10."

By this time, she and Dresden had fallen for one another and shared the same bedroom, which left them with an open room. Sharon jokingly said, "Too bad you aren't out here. We could split the rent again."

"Yeah, too bad I don't have a job out there," I said.

After a pause, she said, "Actually, I could probably get you a job at Halloween Adventure, if you're serious."

Halloween Adventure, the year-round Halloween store in midtown Manhattan, was where Sharon worked. The prospect of a new job made something turn in my head, and I seriously considered moving somewhere else for the first time in my life. Growing up, I always pictured that I would spend my late teens and early twenties serving a Mormon mission and then going to college before getting married; I canceled the mission when I stopped going to church, had just dropped out of school, and wasn't even close to dating anyone, much less marrying. I didn't have any concrete prospects left. The main reason I was still at Western Wats—one of the five longest-tenured dialers by this point—was because I regarded job interviews, if I could even get to that point with my threadbare resume, as foregone failure. On the spot, I told Sharon that I would go out and give it a trial run if she could get me the job.

That surprised her, and she waited a week to give me a chance to back out. I was again standing on the balcony when she called to see if I was seriously interested. She said there would be a position opening up soon, and she could recommend me if I really did want to move. I looked over at the drummer of Adjacent to the Lord, who was shirtless in a lawn chair, playing his drumsticks on his stomach. I said, "Let me come out and see."

Then I did my best imitation of what Sharon had done: I worked long hours, cut back on nearly all expenses, and saved until I had enough for a flight and a month of shared New York rent. I put in my two weeks' notice at Western Wats. My supervisor seemed stunned when I did so, either because he had pegged me as a lifer, or because he'd forgotten that one could give notice instead of quitting in the customary way of not showing up, dodging his phone calls, and getting a friend to sign for the last paycheck. "Well, Palmer, we're sad to see you go, but you have a job here any time if you come back," he said.

～

It was mainly my mom who was upset with the plan. Even Joe hadn't moved as far as New York City, and he still dropped by Uncle Mike's pretty regularly, even if only when he needed money—a recurrent prodigal son who kept eating the fatted calf, collecting more inheritance, and heading out again.

"What, exactly, are you hoping to find out there?" she asked.

"Myself," I said, but the answer was rote and insincere, and I cringed after saying it.

On the plane, I thought about her question some more, again failing to come up with a satisfying answer. It seemed like the decision should have felt transformational, but it didn't. I knew nothing about

New York beyond what the average consumer of television knew. I wasn't even that dissatisfied with my life in Utah, except that it seemed everyone else was moving on without me. My Mormon friends were on missions or getting engaged; my secular friends were passionate about something—music, art, travel, love, drug use, vandalism. . . .

For Sharon, the plane rising over Great Salt Lake must have felt like she was finally realizing her dreams; by the time she saw the New York City skyline, she must have told herself it was just what she had imagined all along. But I didn't have much idea where I was going. I stared down at the lake from the plane and tried to visualize the future. The image I conjured up was an exaggerated series of adult signifiers such as office chairs and suits, and I could not see myself in them.

∾

When I had spoken with her on the phone, Sharon had often mentioned how different she felt in New York. She said the city was a refuge for runaways and castoffs, and that she'd never felt so connected as she did surrounded by the "like-minded" individuals there. I normally tuned out that portion of our conversations, but as I saw Sharon at the airport, she did look different. She walked toward me with a swagger and confidence that I hadn't seen before. The overall transformation—from my overworked roommate who would come home at 11:00 p.m. and stumble into the kitchen to make a "dinner" consisting of a bowl of Frosted Flakes, to a well-groomed woman, smiling in the morning hours—set off a chain of double-takes that didn't fully stop for the rest of my time there.

Sharon guided me into the city. It was my first time on a subway. I found a spot in the corner where I could set my bags without obstructing anyone's way. Nobody made eye contact with anyone else, and I admired how everyone seemed to know just what they were doing.

∾

Sharon had left work to pick me up, so we went straight back to Halloween Adventure. When we walked out of the subway, fog was covering the city and I could taste the humidity. From television, I felt I had absorbed a pretty good idea of what New York City looked like.

But what sitcom images didn't convey was the smell—a combination of grease, subway steam, and bodies that I found intoxicating right away.

The first thing Sharon did when we entered the building was give directions to some employees. Then she gave me a tour of the store, which was massive—two floors tall, and spanning an entire city block. They sold costumes, makeup, accessories, and more, year-round. Employees on the floor gave people costume ideas and advice; my job would be mainly stocking inventory, occasionally directing a customer to someone else if she mistakenly approached me. "Grunt labor," Sharon called it sheepishly, but it sounded like magnificent, phone-free grunt labor.

At her desk, she opened up the door that held the job applications. "If you think this will work," she said, "you'll just need to fill out one of these."

〜

Sharon worked a long day while I walked around Manhattan, and then we went for dinner. By the time we got back to her apartment in Brooklyn, Dresden was already asleep. Their place was just above Fourth Avenue on Eighteenth Street, on the outskirts of Park Slope: stroller brigades a stone's throw up the hill, and dingy canals made of sentient rust just on the other side of Fourth.

I wondered how the inside of the apartment would look. I knew that they had adopted two cats, and I had a vision of cat hair sticking to old cereal bowls. But Dresden seemed to have taken control of the situation. The apartment smelled like lemon cleaning products, and there was nothing on the floor.

It was a two-bedroom apartment with a tiny garden in the back. On the other side of the garden was a Greek Orthodox Church, the bells of which filled the yard with sound every hour.

The apartment also had a cellar-like underground area that you could access by lifting up a wooden door outside and climbing down a shifty ladder. Nothing was finished down there; moldy shelves and rusty filing cabinets eroded on cold concrete. That area, dank and neglected, more closely resembled our old apartment.

~

That night, Sharon took me out to her favorite bar in Brooklyn. The space was filled with a dreamlike purple lighting. Sharon liked it mainly because the bartender knew her and never carded her, a courtesy she somehow extended to me as well—even though I was practically giggling from the illicit overload of what we were doing. When we walked in, she greeted Sharon with a big hug and placed a straw in each of our mouths.

"The first rule of an orgy: have something in your mouth at all times," she said.

That was my first drink in a bar, my first drink with an umbrella in it, and my first orgy-related advice. Sharon and I reminisced about Adjacent to the Lord and the apartment, as if those had been great times.

After a while, two of her friends, Ruby and Jennifer, joined us.

After she found out where I was from, Ruby asked, "Are you Mormon?"

I said, "Kind of."

"All right then," she said.

I was prepared to be defensive about my home state, but I quickly found that nobody from the East Coast seemed to have any concrete impressions about Utah at all. My impressions of New York may have been founded mostly on stock images from television, but the people I met in New York didn't seem to have even those of the West. The Mormon stereotype I was familiar with—that of a khaki-bedecked, ice cream-loving do-gooder who speaks in exclamation points—while reductive, is nevertheless not all that different from many people you'll meet if you spend a day walking around Provo. But in New York City, nobody even had that starting point. They seemed to have just stuffed Mormonism in the compartment of weird religions, and knew Utah was one of the states with lots of right angles—a heartland-ish region swarming with rosy-cheeked Republicans. Sometimes people said, "I hear it's beautiful there"; once, I was asked, "So, do they have, like, horses there?" But generally, people just nodded and changed the subject.

∼

I officially met Dresden the next morning—a Saturday. At breakfast, Dresden asked Sharon—"Babe"—if she would like to try some eggs, while holding a fork full of them toward Sharon's face. She talked about how poorly she had slept and how her allergies were acting up. Sharon handed her a Kleenex, and then, after she used it, Dresden handed it back and Sharon threw it away. From there, Dresden spent a good portion of the morning talking about how much she despised tourists, complaining of their clueless idiocy; it was hard not to take her comments personally.

Not to say Dresden was a downer. Discounting her hatred of allergies and tourists, she was actually the opposite, and then some—a parody of enthusiasm. We walked to Prospect Park after breakfast, and I stopped in my tracks when I noticed that she was walking down the sidewalk with her arm linked in Sharon's, yellow brick road-style. Perhaps she thought I had paused due to feeling excluded, because she linked my arm into the chain. When we got to the park, she delightedly kicked the leaves in the air as she walked.

Her fervor confused and lightly annoyed me, but I kept it to myself both for reasons of standard roommate repression and because I was afraid she would attribute my contempt to red state homophobia. Besides, Sharon seemed to like it. Dresden and Sharon looked out for one another, and functioned at a surprisingly high level, considering Sharon had once tried to avoid arguing with a girl by asking me to tell her that Sharon no longer lived at our apartment and nobody knew where she'd gone.

That was the dynamic between us throughout my time in New York. I saw that Dresden made Sharon happy, for some reason, so I daily renewed a vow not to interfere, and tried to avoid fights. But right away I felt like a houseguest who had overstayed his welcome. The apartment was cozy, and there wasn't much happening there except for intolerable cutesiness. For example: Dresden and Sharon were obsessed with the two cats—Guinevere and Galileo—even though all they did all day was brush their rusty heads against the bars in the windows. When feeding the cats, instead of saying nothing, they would ask: "Who's a hungry, hungry hippo?" Even the cats seemed to roll their eyes at the question, but they were asked every time.

～

Partially to avoid going home, partially because I felt electrified by the trains and bridges, I spent most days walking and riding the subway until well past sundown. I ate nothing but pizza slices. I found that my slim body and long legs moved well within the density of New York; I could cut and swerve around slower pedestrians without making contact, and easily weave around stopped or still-moving cars.

Sharon pressured me to commit to the job, as she couldn't keep it open forever. But I kept putting her off. It was as if I could answer her only after walking everywhere.

To the extent that I had a social life, I fell in with Dresden and Sharon's crowd, which mostly consisted of artists and musicians in their twenties. Everyone liked Dresden and Sharon as a couple, and tolerated me at Sharon's behest.

Being the only male at a table of smart, creative women was a scenario I would have thought impossible during my high school years of sobriety, trombone practice, and acne. Unfortunately, I knew nothing about art, and did not genuinely enjoy many of the activities the artists did. This was the kind of crowd that, on a Saturday, liked to go to the Farmer's Market followed by a trip to the Brooklyn Museum to see the new collection of Colonial furniture. In such situations, I tried to imitate how I felt a mature person would act, reading bronze placards and trying to keep my eyes from glazing over while thinking, *There was plenty of old furniture to stare at back home.*

Dresden always went to bed early. She pronounced hard alcohol "icky," and added that she "grew up in an area [note: upstate New York] where we had more to do than just get drunk."

～

I was never really bored, but I was much more homesick than I expected. Once, in a move so out-of-character it must have been fueled by desperation, I approached some sister missionaries who had just exited the Staten Island Ferry. After I found out that one of them was from Sandy, not far from my hometown, I detained them with questions about Utah for so long that, for likely the first time in their missions, they were the ones who had to make polite excuses about having places to be.

It surprised me how easily Sharon was able to embrace New York and forget about Utah. Her favorite activities back home, not counting drinking Keystone Light on the balcony, had been "doing doughnuts" in empty parking lots in the winter and hiking in the summer. When Utah Lake froze, we'd walk down there and she would run across its surface, while I waited on the shore. She always had more courage.

~

One Sunday, I woke up to the sound of rain. I decided, as usual, to take a walk. Sharon told me not to leave without an umbrella, but I ignored her.

In Utah, when it rains, the rain is light and makes you more irritated than wet. On the rare occasions when it does come down hard, it passes fast. But in New York City, I was to find out, such deluges could last all day. That morning, already soaked through just from walking to the subway, I tried to take refuge in the Brooklyn Heights stop until the rain let up. But it never did, and I didn't want to go home. I decided that I would just keep going.

I was drenched, but not cold. It was by far the emptiest I'd ever seen the city. The previous sunny Sunday, as Sharon, Dresden, and I had walked back to the apartment over the Brooklyn Bridge, it was full of bikers and joggers and walkers. This time I saw a single man stretching a garbage bag over his head, his sneakers thumping on the wood. The rain was falling fast and heavy. I saw water in the sky and below me—contrasts of gray blurring together from the buildings to the horizon to the water. If not for the solid wood beneath my feet, I would have felt totally disoriented.

I stayed at the middle of the bridge for a long time. The rain blurred my vision, but I could see faint outlines of the orange ferries heading to Staten Island—fireflies on the distance. Immediately, it felt like one of those sights I wouldn't forget the rest of my life, a notion I tried to wave off because it made no sense. But I never have forgotten it. When I think about it now, the memory is imbued with nostalgia, but if nostalgia is what I felt at the time, it was premature. I had no conscious plans to leave New York, but on some level, I must have known that I wasn't going to make it there.

That night, after I changed out of my sopping clothes, I called my mom. She talked about what happened in church that day, and a hike up Battlecreek Canyon she had taken with the dog that afternoon. I used to dread phone conversations with her because of tedious details just like those, but from far away I found myself listening closely. I asked her, "What else can you tell me about the hike?" It wasn't just call-center tactics. I genuinely wanted to know more.

~

The conscious realization that I wasn't going to make it came not long thereafter. Sharon, who had started playing her guitar on the subway, had written a song about Utah and Mormonism that included the lines, "Glad I'm off that track / Never goin' back." She played it for Dresden and me in the kitchen. I was not as supportive as I could have been, calling the song "the worst thing I've heard since we lived next to Adjacent to the Lord." Sharon laughed it off, but my remark incensed Dresden. "What kind of friend are you?" she asked. I didn't answer, and she took my silence as an opportunity to excoriate me for ten minutes. Sharon tried to cut her off a few times, but she said, "No, he needs to hear this."

The overall theme of her lecture was friendship, but she freely digressed to take jabs at my single/virginal status, directionless future, and overall "sourpuss" attitude along the way. When she was done, I was too stunned to retaliate. I walked outside and sulked down the rickety ladder to the cellar area just to get away from them for a while, and have some space to myself—albeit a dismal, subterranean space. Unfortunately, I forgot to bring my pipe with me, and had to walk back up into the tension and retrieve it. Nobody said anything. Back in the cellar, I got high and nearly fell asleep leaning against the cold cement wall. When I finally climbed back up, I silently walked into my room and started looking up in-state tuition rates in Utah.

~

When I told her I was leaving, Sharon tried to talk me out of it. At first, she was conciliatory, and then she grew angry. "I opened up my home and held that job for you," she said, "and you repay me by running back to that shithole state. Nice. Don't you have any ambition? At all?"

"Look, I'm sorry you came all this way to shack up with a moron," I said. "If that's all you wanted to do with your life, you could've stayed home. We have plenty."

Leading up to my departure, most of our intra-apartment communication took place via loudly-closed doors. On the day I left, Sharon rode the subway with me to the airport, but said nothing the whole way.

"Good luck," she said before I got on the bus for La Guardia.

"You too," I said.

~

I moved home, and took out a loan to pay for a semester of tuition at Utah Valley State College. Having dropped out of college, then out of New York, I was right back where I started. My prodigal return even reestablished Joe as the official family warning story, with my brief exodus no more than a footnote.

Part of me had hoped New York would change me on its own, and it did—in small ways. Whenever steam hit my nose, I still had hallucinatory flashes of tall buildings and water. But overall, the experience felt like a vivid dream I was awakened from and couldn't get back to because I had to get on with my mundane day. The further away I got from the experience, the dimmer the images seemed. But they never faded out entirely. Riding the bus to school one rainy day, the person I was sitting next to said, "It's really coming down out there." I heard myself saying the last sentence that a bus rider in Utah would ever want to hear, but I couldn't prevent it from happening: "You know, when I lived in New York. . . ."

~

I had a new roommate, a backslapping Muscle Milk fanatic who was good-natured but made me miss Sharon on a regular basis. One night, I decided I would call her. To prepare, I wrote up an apology script that admittedly emphasized more that I had abandoned the job she'd found for me and less that I had insulted Dresden. Thankfully, when I called, she didn't make me read it. I started, "Look, I'm sorry about..." and she said, "Hey, don't worry about it. Me too." And, like everything else in my life, our relationship reset.

When I talked to her on the phone after that, she made it a custom to pause in the middle of her stories to add, "When you come back, you'll see what I'm talking about."

I said, "Maybe you're right." And then she'd continue telling me about Dresden, Halloween Adventure, the bridges, the weather, the pizza, the buildings, and everything she'd done that weekend.

And I would ask her what else she could tell me about that.

"And what else?"

# Legend

As soon as Milo got shot in the eye with his own BB gun, he grew into the persona of someone cool enough to have a glass eye.

It was the only glass eye any of us had ever seen, and Milo was much more popular with it than he had been with two real ones. The BB seemed to have changed something inside him, as well. Milo dyed his hair bright red with Kool Aid, the first in our school to do something like that. In church or school, he would simply walk away from his responsibilities and go outside.

I coveted his eye. If I had it, I would use it to stare where weaker eyes, such as mine, couldn't—to never flinch from any challenge, to look straight at the sun. I held my hand over my left eye to see if I could be okay with just one eye's vision. *Definitely*, I thought.

I also wanted his transformation. Milo had been just another boy and then one day he was a superhero cyclops.

I also wanted Milo to get revenge on Aaron, the boy who shot him. I once lost a fight to Aaron in church. By the end of it, he was beating me with a set of scriptures—Old Testament, New Testament, Book of Mormon, Doctrine & Covenants, and Pearl of Great Price, all in one thick book. Not any set of scriptures, but my own set, which were held in a soft blue leather case with a blue handle for swinging. I had never forgiven him for that. Nor had I done anything about it. I wanted Milo to take the vengeance baton from me.

But he didn't. Once, on the playground, I asked him if he ever felt mad at Aaron for what he'd done. He told me that it had been an accident, so why would he be mad? I shrugged. He looked me over in silence.

"If your right eye offends," he said after a while, "you know what to do." He winked over his glass eye.

# Vacuum Specialist

I was back home from New York by early December. My parents picked me up at the airport. On the ride home, they sat up front and I sat in the back. Our conversation was about how nice it was to see Christmas lights, and how high up people were building on the mountain. They didn't ask anything about my time in New York, I didn't volunteer anything, and it was understood by all of us that my time there was going to be a brief mistake I needed to silently move on from.

There was some inverted pollution trapped in the Salt Lake valley, and soft curls of white smoke gave the snow a hazy, cottony blur. It looked like a snow globe. Only when we exited the freeway in Pleasant Grove did I notice how much it had snowed—plows had formed walls of snow nearly as tall as I was alongside the roads.

When we got home, I said hello to my sisters and then carried my bags downstairs into my old room. There were a few new pictures on the wall, mostly of my brother in his suit and nametag, taken just before he left for Ecuador to serve a Mormon mission. My mother had painted over the various lyrics and slogans I had written in marker on the walls of my room, though you could still see hints of words—"Straight Edge for Life," "At Least I Can Think," "Against All Authority"— if you looked closely. With the slogans painted over, the room had a ghostly, institutional quality, as if it had been prepared for a new son to move in. Instead, it got a slightly older version of the same one.

Back in my old bedroom, the lack of progress I'd made as an adult to that point closed in on me. It was as if I had stayed still for the past two and a half years—twenty years old but no different than I was when I graduated high school. Since then, I had completed one year of college, with bad enough grades that I lost my scholarship and had to drop out. I had gone to New York looking for purpose, but found myself lonely and out of place; I never engaged with the city the way true adventurers are supposed to. And even though it had been years since I'd stopped going to church, I was still a virgin.

Virginity was one thing in high school. I had a brutal case of acne at the time, and no ability to think of anything but that when talking to anyone. But by this time the acne's only remnant was some scarring on my shoulders, and I had pretty eyes and was skinny. In the reflection of bus windows, I looked handsome enough to almost convince myself that I was the person I wished I was. If any of the New York stories were true, uglier, less charming guys than me were definitely getting laid. At the same time, I had lain in bed under the covers with a girl named Melissa, and held perfectly still until we talked ourselves to sleep.

Growing up, I always assumed I would lose my virginity on my wedding night, and though I outwardly cited the possibility of premarital sex as one of the big perks of not going to church, it didn't actually feel like one. I hadn't learned much from New York, except that in temperament, I was basically just a Mormon who never went to church—especially when I didn't have enough money for booze or drugs. Though I learned to talk a decent game about the importance of sex-positive paradigms, inwardly I was still shocked by the sexual openness of my peers there, who could talk about their bedroom experiences in well-lit places during normal daytime hours without hushed tones.

Not only did I feel like I would be a virgin forever, I felt uncertain whether I wanted to change that or not. Some of my conflict probably owed to the effectiveness of abstinence rhetoric. Thanks to some visual aids, I knew they told girls that, as virgins, they were born peaches—but after having sex became a rotten peach. That message seemed to be for girls primarily, but the image of rotten fruit was a lasting one. I remembered the advice given to me by my uncle to ensure that I would stay pure until it was time to go on a mission: *Just tell yourself that she's cut down there.* When I was thirteen, I was slipped a pamphlet about how to quit masturbating that included the advice to think of festering worms every time you felt aroused. My friend Brad, who claimed to have slept with Mary, "among others," told me that sex was just "lust and hormones, man," but it felt much bigger than that. I never would have admitted it out loud because I knew the kinds of eye rolls such a melodramatic pronouncement would trigger, but I felt that any path I chose was going to lead to a regret I could never undo, whether that meant staying a virgin forever, getting married for the wrong reason, or having sex and feeling like a rotten peach afterward. And even that line of thinking ignored the reality that nobody was lining up outside my bedroom to make the dilemma real.

$\sim$

I applied online for a job as a "vacuum specialist" at Utah Valley State College, the school where I'd lost my scholarship. They needed someone right away, after the last guy had been fired for sleeping on the job. The manual instructing me how to use the vacuum was already on the desk when I showed up for my interview. I'm not sure what it would have taken for them to not hire me, and I was relieved. It kept me out of the call center. I worked eight-hour shifts; two four-hour blocks with one hour for lunch in-between. The smoky December dusks seemed to always arrive right as my shift ended, and I'd ride the bus home in the dark.

During my lunch break, I would walk to the Sinclair gas station across the street from campus and get coffee and a sandwich for lunch. A few on-campus restaurants were still open, and the gas station smelled of sulfur, but I didn't want to see anyone I recognized and have to answer how classes were going.

One day on my walk to the gas station, a slant of sunshine moved between clouds. It felt as if I hadn't seen the sun in days, and I felt warm instantly, despite the actual temperature. The sun also began to melt the snow weighing down the branches; heaps of it softly thumped the sidewalk below. The salt sprinkled over the sidewalks glimmered, the sidewalk looking like a magic path showing me the way. I ate my lunch at my usual table in the gas station.

I was vacuuming the basement of the liberal arts building later that afternoon when Anna stopped me. She had dark brown hair, dark brown eyes, and a black hoodie. I was stunned when she interrupted my vacuuming; usually that only happened when someone wanted to point out that the portable vacuums we carried on our backs looked like jetpacks, or the backpacks from *Ghostbusters*. I was somewhat familiar with Anna from my days as a student; we had one class together, an ancient civilizations class, in which we were once placed in the same small group assigned to give a presentation on Egypt. I still had her phone number, given to me for the purposes of that project. I had called it just once—a superfluous call, ostensibly related to our class. She still lived at home, and during our conversation, she had been distracted by something her sister was doing and mostly talked to her.

In the hallway, she asked what I'd been up to. I pretended that my time in New York had been more exciting than it was, but that I regrettably had to move home to go back to school. We talked about what we were doing over the holidays—both of us staying in town with family. She told me to give her a call if I wanted to commiserate about it, and then walked away. After she was about twenty feet away, she turned around and said, "Nice vacuum, by the way."

~

Pushed by the desperation and boredom of spending all my time in my parents' basement, I did find the courage to call her. I took the cordless phone out to the basketball hoop where no one could hear me, and we talked about her summer trip to visit family in North Carolina. The lightning storms were unlike anything she had ever seen.

I began skipping lunch at the Sinclair in hopes of running into her. It never worked—it was still Christmas break, and she was probably just picking something up that one time—but somehow eating a peanut-butter-and-jelly sandwich alone in an empty classroom was less bleak than the gas station. In the evening, over AOL Messenger, I talked to Anna about how strange it was to be in a classroom when no one was there—devoid of conversation, the bare-bones construction of the liberal arts building really stood out.

"If you want," she said, "I'll come eat with you next week."

~

I chose the nicest room in the building that day—one on the second floor with a view of the parking lot. Anna met me there, with an egg salad sandwich in glass Tupperware that she brought from home. She was again wearing a black hoodie and this time a lot of mascara.

"So, how many brothers and sisters do you have?" I asked, unable to think of anything better.

"One brother, four sisters. You?"

"One and two."

"Mormon, I'm guessing?"

"Oh, yeah. You?"

"Since the days of Brother Brigham."

"Yeah. Do you have big Christmas plans?"

"Not really. Everyone's grown except one sister, and she's seventeen."

"Same. What will you do for Christmas now that nobody's a kid?"

"We'll just pretend we still are, and do it the same as always."

~

About a week before Christmas, after my shift vacuuming, my mom asked me if I was ready for "another crazy night" at Aunt Andrea's. I'd forgotten about that tradition, which involved all of the relatives on my mom's side of the family getting together for singing and games and a re-enacted nativity.

"Oh, I don't think I can go this year," I said.

"Why not?" she said.

"I'm just a little tired after work. . . . "

"Well, you haven't been going out much lately. I just thought it might be nice for you to get out."

That was true: All I did when I wasn't working was brood in the basement, call Anna, or go for long walks uphill toward the mountains; as far as I could get before I got too cold or tired.

"Yeah, I know. But I don't know if this is the best night."

"I see. It's just that with your brother gone, it might be nice to try to do something as a family. What family we have here, anyway. And you weren't able to go last year. . . ." "All right, I'll go."

Because I had forgotten about the party, I had saved myself from having to dread it all month; but now that it was near, the full horror of the party drenched me at once. Every year, families brought plates of cookies or brownies and descended down the stairs into Andrea's basement-turned-preschool-turned-party headquarters, with Mickey Mouse illustrations teaching kids how to count still lining the perimeter of the walls. Families would perform musical numbers or skits, and then child actors would re-enact the nativity. As an added bonus for adulthood, I assumed the festivities would be followed by questions about what I was doing with my life.

On the way, we picked up my great aunt Ina, a name that registered with me in language only—no face or even blurred image. She was old and her husband had passed away earlier in the year, so she was going to spend the holidays with us.

Her house in American Fork was tidy, but dusty. A black cat walked around the corner. "I put the catnip out for that little devil, and he just rolled over in it," Ina said. She fed the cat; we locked the door and left.

In the car, Aunt Ina asked about my brother, and how his mission was going. My dad started to answer. For my part, I hardly ever wrote him, and didn't really know how he was. His first letter to me from Ecuador was a detailed description of a celebration that involved the burning of effigies—he noted the size, heat, and brightness of the fires all around—but his e-mails from there became more focused on the proselytizing efforts, and it was hard to get motivated to write him when I knew he would eventually turn that gaze my way. I was thinking about what I might say to him in my next letter when Ina managed to turn around in her seat and look at me. "How long until we're going to have another missionary in the family?" she asked. I mumbled something unintelligible—but in a bright tone—and looked out the window. My dad changed the subject. I could hear the wind outside; snow whirled around the car and seemed to move back up into the sky.

~

The snow slowed the commute, and it was dark when we parked on the street a few houses down. We walked into the house, down its throat to the congested basement, warm from excessive laughter and too many bodies. We were just in time to catch the other Michael (my cousin) playing "Silent Night" on the piano.

Since we were late and there was already musical entertainment in the room, my mom wouldn't feel pressure to provide a family musical number of our own, which put me more at ease. Other Michael finished, and it looked like the nativity was next. Kids were herded into the storage room to prepare the re-enactment. From the age of six until the age of twelve—the minimum cutoff year for kids no longer required to participate—I was the wise man who brought Jesus a plastic treasure chest of gold in that pageant. Joseph had always been reserved for Other Michael. The angel wings were too sparkly for boys, the barn animals had been rendered unnecessary since the year my cousin Seth became overzealous with his part and kicked a dent in the piano, and my cousins Beth and Aslen insisted on taking two of the three shepherd parts every year because they liked pretending to eat the giant candy canes they used for canes. That left the option of the third shepherd and the wise men. But gold wise man was by far the best role of them all. *Would you like to bring frankincense or myrrh to Jesus?* Aunt Andrea would sometimes ask while adjusting someone's angel wings. *No, thank you.* Gold wise man had no lines, and the least complicated costume—a round red hat and a plastic treasure chest. The other two wise men had purple, Hugh Heffner-style robes, and they had to carry around fragile ornaments that someone once imagined could hold frankincense or myrrh. All I had to do was leave the chest at Cabbage Patch Jesus's plastic feet at the appropriate time, and then I could lean into the background and start counting down the minutes, knowing the worst was over.

I didn't recognize most of the child actors this year. Andrea's husband Darrell always read the Bible version of the birth of Christ. (There's a version of the same story in the Book of Mormon.) While he read, I was thinking through a litany of unrelated things: when we were going to get out of there, if I would ever have sex, what I was going to do when we got home, and my brother in Ecuador. I wondered how long it would take him to be engaged when he got home, guessed it would probably take about six months. I imagined his fiancée: Her name would be Annette. She would be a Timpview High graduate who now went to BYU. She would have strawberry blonde hair and freckles and would enjoy dancing, including ballroom and country line dancing, which my brother would eventually also take up, "charm" compensating for his linebacker build and lack of finesse. They would meet in a singles ward. My brother would notice her during church, then talk to her during a weekly activity involving stilts. He would mention to her that he was taking night classes at UVSC and working full-time in order to become financially and academically eligible for BYU. He would say that he wanted to go into real estate, that he had a true testimony of the church, the strength of which he only discovered on his mission. She would look into his brown eyes, see that he meant it.

It was impossible for me to sort out whether those visions were accurate to Matthew's character, or if they were holdovers from when I used to fantasize about my own marriage as a child. But I knew it was what I used to want. And without that—marriage, church, family—I wasn't sure what to picture.

I was thinking about how he would propose to her—deciding between hiring a horse and carriage and wearing knight-in-shining-armor apparel, or taking her up to the top of Mount Timpanogos and proposing there, as my parents had done—when the scripture ended. The sequence seemed faster than I remembered, and Christ's birth as a whole felt anticlimactic as I had tuned out of most of the buildup. Besides, it was only eight thirty. My dad then went upstairs and brought down a dozen roses that he had been hiding somewhere and presented them to Aunt Ina. He said he remembered how Ina told us her husband Earl presented her with a dozen roses every Christmas. Ina started to cry and break everyone's heart, including mine, even though I still had no idea who she was.

After we felt we had observed the necessary period of looking at our feet in silence, my older cousins and uncles started gathering around the chips and brownies to debate the hire of Bronco Mendenhall as BYU's new football coach, or whether the Jazz, without a star post-Stockton and Malone, had a chance at making the playoffs that year.

43

The kids hovered around the Christmas tree investigating gifts. My mom was laughing with some of the other moms and my sisters were coercing Other Michael to play another number on the piano. My dad stuck by Ina. I didn't know what to do with myself. Most years I would have staked out a corner with my brother, and waited it out until mom was ready to go. The rest of my immediate family was detained. I loved to talk about the Jazz, but my cousins and uncles were prone to unnecessary hand-on-the-shoulder advice when talking to someone younger, especially someone not committed to going on a mission, so I crossed that possibility off and waited by myself on the couch.

After a few minutes, one of my aunts appeared next to me. Her arrival was cartoonishly sudden for anyone, especially a person holding a baby in her arms and pregnant with another.

"Would you like to hold her?"

"Actually, thank you, but I am not that good with babies. Thank you, though."

"Come on, go ahead and hold her. She likes you!" she said, and lifted the baby up to my face, as if that were proof.

"Wow, she is really adorable. But actually, I don't know, I don't really know how," I said.

"Come on, here you are," she said, and handed the child over. "There, see? She likes you!" My aunt stood up and left me. I held the baby in my arms and stared into her face. She was surprisingly heavy for a baby. Her body was warm and spongy. She smiled, and it was cute. My aunt was probably on the opposite side of the house by now and I knew that I would be looking into the baby's face until she started crying or until my mom stopped "visiting" and was ready to go—and I wasn't sure what to do about that. Put my thick, villainous eyebrows to use and start making scary faces at her, hoping she would react badly and have to be taken away by someone more competent? Start trying to make eye contact with my mom, who might realize my discomfort and feel she owed me one for coming in the first place and break away from visiting a little earlier than usual? Instead, I stared at the baby and she stared back. I stared at her and she stared back.

We continued like that for a while, until I was glad to have her. . . . . Her presence gave me the appearance of having something to do. My mom finally came by and picked the baby up. She was still wearing her Christmas sweater and I wondered how she wasn't sweating in the basement's infernal heat. Once she found someone to take the baby, we left. I emerged from the stuffy basement, waved goodbye without making eye contact, moved fast to the coat pile, and finally walked out the door and into the cold, black winter air, which felt new, and open.

～

When we got back to my parents' house, I went straight down into the basement. It was still early—just after nine thirty—and I was not at all tired. I looked over the VHS tapes down there; before my brother left for his mission, he had purged the house of all movies with any hint of bad language, sex, or violence, and now my viewing choices were limited to Disney movies, The Sound of Music, or Little House on the Prairie.

I took the cordless phone downstairs and called Anna to see what she was doing. She answered and said her family had just finished their nightly scripture study. I told her about Andrea's party and she asked if I wanted to get a cup of coffee. This felt like a big step—the first time we'd be in the same place at night—and I responded to the question the way a benchwarmer not expecting to play might. I said, "Uh, well, all right." Did I have a car? No, but maybe I could get one.

I went upstairs and told my mom that Brad was having some people over to his new house in Orem. In truth, he was currently living with his sister in the same house he grew up in, but she didn't know that. Because Brad wasn't in the ward, she couldn't track his activities.

"I don't know, it's supposed to get kind of bad out there," she said, looking out the window.

Seizing an opportunity, I said, "I'll be careful. If it gets too bad, I'll stay the night over there."

She thought about it, and then I reversed the guilt she had used on me earlier to talk about how I finally wanted to leave the house, and for once, I really felt like it. "I'll be back before midnight, unless the roads are too bad, and then I'll just stay the night. I'll be sure to call," I said.

She moved her head to the side, her signal for the reluctant go-ahead.

~

I'm not sure what Anna told her parents, if anything, but she was already standing outside in the snow when I picked her up. She had likely been out there a while, as I wasn't used to Lehi, which is on the north end of the valley, close to the point of the mountain, and it took me a while to find her house. I asked her if she was cold and she said, "A little." I turned up the heat and drove her to Denny's. The music there was country Christmas covers.

We talked mostly about our families, and about church. Like me, she hadn't been for a few years, didn't have much faith left, but felt defensive about the religion because her family was so devout.

"I know," I said. "Even though my heart isn't in it, it feels like an arm or leg or something still is," I said.

"I recommend cutting that back to no more than a toe," she said.

We got three refills and an English muffin each, before the waitress told us her shift was almost over, and hinted that maybe ours should be too. Anna asked me if I wanted to go look at the lights, and I called my mom from Anna's cell phone and told her I was going to spend the night at Brad's. Anna called her house and told her own story—but I don't know what it was, since she made the call outside while I was paying the five-dollar check.

After Denny's, we drove around for a while. My family's Astro van was terrible in the snow, and I panicked every time it slid diagonally toward a stoplight. Thankfully, the roads were nearly empty. The neon colors of State Street were absorbed by the snow between tire tracks. Still, I was desperate for a place to stop. There was too much snow on the ground to reach the summer canyon spots. Anna knew of a backroad that wound above the Lindon cemetery, but that was closed off as well. I didn't really want to drive the van on neighborhood roads that might not have been plowed and salted.

We eventually made our way to the summit where you could hike to either the G on the mountain or to the waterfall. That the Astro van made it up there was a Christmas miracle—it fishtailed a couple of times, and I was wondering what I would tell my parents, not to mention Anna's, if the van ended up in a snowbank up there—but I drove steadily and it lurched forward. We made it to the summit, the only ones that high up, and I parked the van facing the city.

Thanks to a grove of trees, that viewpoint only gave glimpses into the city, through the empty branches, and the views shifted and closed with the wind. It was snowing, and I looked through the windshield up into the sky. I kept the van running for the heat and the music. The singer's voice was piercing and sweet and sad, but when I moved to turn it off, Anna stopped me. She offered me some vodka from a flask she kept in her backpack. I hadn't had anything to drink since I'd come home from New York, but that sounded like something I could do and I took a few eye-squinting swigs of it.

The windows were fogging up. I felt the urge to step outside, but didn't move. Anna stood up, and slipped between the front seats into the middle section of the van, which consisted of two more reclining seats. She sat on one of them. "How do you move these back?" she asked, while pulling on the lever. The lever on the seat she was sitting in was broken, but I moved into the back and showed her that the other, root beer-stained seat could lean back. I demonstrated. She moved over to my side and on top of me. We kissed for a while with her knees arcing over my hips. She put her hands under my shirt and her hands were cold as she slid them up and down my chest and ribs. After a few minutes of this I started to feel a scratchy, slow sort of sadness move up my spine, and I thought about the tree branches moving in front of the moon and city. I stopped and she asked, "What's wrong?"

"Nothing," I said, thinking over my options.

I could slow this down. Negotiate my way down the icy hill. The snow would cover my tracks. Maybe Anna wouldn't take it personally; maybe I could explain to her that I felt the urge to get married first; maybe she would understand; maybe she would even marry me. Or I could stay.

I was feeling a buzz from caffeine and alcohol. I could see the snow touch the windows and melt. The night was getting deeper, and the wind was picking up. I didn't want to commit to a decision, so I just looked out the window and tried not to think. It didn't work. I was a virgin in my hometown. I had this choice to make.

Anna squeezed my hand and said, "Chill. Have some more vodka."

All I knew from how seduction happened I learned from movies—and often those scenes shifted to montage as soon as they got started. I had no idea what to do, or how one thing could lead to another, how leaving my hand on her shoulder could lead to her sliding it under her shirt, how her hair could drip onto my face, how I could feel the smoothness of her back, how she would awkwardly help me get my shirt off, and we both had goosebumps, the sight of which caused me to move to the front to crank the van's heat higher, how she would get a condom out of her backpack as I did so, and we would return to where we were, with her on top of me, how all the windows would fog up and we hoped we were the only ones stupid enough to drive where we were, how she could laugh about it afterward but not in a cruel way, and then we could talk for the rest of the night because both of us had said we were spending the night elsewhere and neither of us could go home.

# Salesman

That summer I sold knives. While vacuuming, I noticed the orange flyers posted throughout the college—they looked like advertisements for a Halloween dance. $12.50 an hour just for making appointments. No door-to-door. Get paid without selling. No experience required.

I took a flyer and told Brad, who was unemployed, about it. We attended the information session later that week.

The Vector Marketing headquarters were in a strip mall in south Orem, and we could smell the fumes of the Chinese restaurant nearby as we walked through the glass doors. We were greeted in the lobby by two white men, both wearing blue button-down shirts. Brad and I must have been the last to arrive because they started their spiel as soon as we sat down.

We would call people to set up appointments—and get paid for doing so. Even better, we wouldn't be cold-calling strangers, but people we already had a connection with. During the scheduled appointment, we really just needed to present the already-written script to the customer. If we did that, we'd get paid. If we sold some products while there, we would make even more, but we got paid regardless. What were we selling? "High quality kitchen products." How much would we make? "That's up to you. But truly, the sky's the limit." But the $12.50 per appointment was guaranteed? "Of course." Passing out the applications afterward, they reminded us that these positions were highly competitive.

As Brad and I walked up to the desk to hand in our applications, one of the presenters cut us off.

"Guys, I sense a lot of potential here. But why don't you come back next week, when you're dressed a little more professionally. In the meantime, I'll hang on to these," he said.

I was wearing a collared shirt, which was the nicest thing I'd ever worn outside of a church. My clothing might have passed had

Brad not been there; his jeans had a hole in the left knee and he was wearing a black Alkaline Trio T-shirt with a skull on it.

We walked to the food court in University Mall and ate some Panda Express while we brooded over our shared rejection. Brad summarized the experience as a "pageant of pyramid scheme dipshits," but even as he said it, I could tell he was resigning himself to putting on a suit and returning. For one thing, he didn't have any other options. For another, I think we were both seduced by the idea of making a lot of money fast. (Not that we would have admitted it.) I kept my job as vacuum specialist, but I came back with him. I made $8 an hour vacuuming. For a moment, I allowed myself to dream of actual money, of the trainers' promised sky.

~

When I returned the next week, I wore a short-sleeved white dress shirt, slacks, and a blue tie. I looked exactly like a Mormon missionary, including the backpack, and if my life had gone as I had thought it would, I would have been finishing a mission instead of selling knives.

Brad wore a baggy suit, likely borrowed from his father, and this time they accepted our applications. The next day, they called and invited us to training.

It was unpaid training, and I had to take time off from my other job to attend. Eight of us were there—seven men and one woman, all between about nineteen and twenty-five. There were doughnuts and hot chocolate set up on a table in front of the office, and we were told to get comfortable and enjoy. We chomped on the doughnuts for a few minutes until a man pulled up in a silver, convertible Porsche with a vanity plate. It pains me that I can't remember the precise lettering of the plate, but it had some spelling of the word SALES on it.

The man stepped out of the car and took off his sunglasses to appraise us clearly. He wore a fancy suit and had the clean-cut, bright face of a child. His teeth were so white that it seemed he ate coral. After looking us over, he delivered enthusiastic, hot-chocolate-spilling high-fives all around.

"My name is Phil and I am absolutely psyched to be here!" he said. "Come on everyone; follow me!"

We followed him through the lobby, into a conference room, and sat down in the rows of plastic chairs. In the front of the room, many of the Cutco products were displayed atop a red blanket on a long table. Knives of all sizes, a potato peeler, an ice cream scoop, scissors—all gleaming under the fluorescent lighting.

"I am so happy to be here!" Phil said as he took off his jacket. "Soon, ladies and gentlemen, you'll have your own kits with many of these items." He did a "behold" gesture with his arms. That's where we learned that we would have to buy our own kits in order to perform the demonstrations—but at an "amazing" discount. "The discount alone will make you glad you're here. These products will last you the rest of your life."

Brad tried to whisper something and Phil said, "Gentlemen! Is there a question?"

"Just wondering when we can start making money, boss," Brad said.

"A prudent concern!" he said with a smile. "And very soon. Speaking of money, who can tell me what profession makes the most today?"

Someone raised his hand and said, "Doctor?"

"Actually, no! Doctors do very well for themselves, but they aren't number one. Who else?"

"Lawyers?"

"Another good guess, and another fine profession! But not number one. Who else?"

". . . Sales?"

"Ding ding ding! Most people don't know it, but you can actually make more money as a salesman than anything else. With the right effort, the sky's the limit. It's entirely up to you."

Phil then performed a sample demonstration with the knives. In his hands and words, they truly did seem amazing. He handled the items like a magician. The black, ergonomic handles looked sexy in his hands. When he twisted the Petite Chef in the conference room light and asked us to picture using one of these babies on a watermelon, it

really did seem like our watermelon-cutting nightmares were about
to end. Phil cut through pieces of rope and leather like butter. He
used the scissors to cut through a penny.

We made sounds to indicate how impressed we were. "These
products sell themselves, if you can just get the appointments. I'm
telling you: If you can get in the house, the rest of it will take care of
itself."

～

"What a fucking tool," Brad said as we walked down the Provo/
Orem hill toward our apartments. I didn't argue, but I was wondering
what would happen if I actually listened to someone like Phil for
once. I always went to the Brads of the world for guidance, the kinds
of characters who would get stabbed in the second act of a play for
speaking truth to power/annoying some prince. I was still looking
for a post-Mormon life philosophy that I could feel in my blood and
not just agree with. Brad himself had always seemed freer than I,
in part because he seemed to always believe in what he was saying
and doing. In high school, he had missed tons of classes, saying he
didn't want to miss out on "more authentic" experiences by chaining
himself to a classroom desk. His present tack—that there were many
ways to get an education besides college—was similar. I agreed with
him—though it seemed that his major in the School of Life thus far
would have been Finding Drugs with a minor in Never Shutting the
Fuck Up—but I felt his philosophy with a dead man's hand.

And anyway, it wasn't as though I felt a rush of authenticity or
integrity every time I vacuumed a classroom. What if I could spend
that same four-hour shift doing something else I didn't want to do,
but make two-hundred dollars instead of thirty-two? So Phil was a
tool. He was a tool with a car and a dentist, and while Brad might
have been freer than I, it was very possible that Phil was, too.

～

I decided to pay attention in training. I took notes on everything.
According to Phil, here are the keys to setting appointments and
selling knives: Follow the script. Smile. Create a sense of urgency. You
want to let your customer know that you are committed to your goal

52

and have a deadline. If you show that the demo is important to you, they won't reschedule on you at the last minute. While scheduling appointments, don't overemphasize Cutco or sales. Do emphasize that you get paid just for keeping the appointment, that you would really appreciate it if they could help you out. "Cutco is incredible, but they won't understand just how great it is until they see it!" When scheduling, offer them two possible times—"Would Thursday at 6:00 or Saturday at 10:00 be better for you?" Make sure the time really works, and emphasize that you are counting on it. The wife is often easier to schedule than the husband. When keeping the appointment, don't call ahead of time; just show up. If they don't answer, don't leave a message. Instead, call again immediately afterward so they know it's important. Make sure you are in a quiet place when you call. In person, avoid silence. Silences lead to people saying, "Well, you've given me a lot to think about. I'll let you know. . . ." Silence was effective only after asking one question: "Would you like to get this set of Cutco today and receive the potato peeler for free?" Be completely quiet and wait for an answer.

Beyond the scripts, the two biggest things I learned from observing Phil: The job was about making yourself likeable and about believing in what you were selling. If customers liked you, they wouldn't find you pushy. If you believed in what you were offering, you wouldn't feel manipulative. Any sales tactic is appropriate if you're saving someone from the lifetime of strain that comes from using mediocre knives. And I don't think Phil ever doubted that he was liked, even when confronted with someone like Brad, who started dreaming of Phil's death before the summer ended.

∾

When I would roleplay with Phil and my fellow prospective salespeople during training, I always knew the right answer. I would just mimic Phil's language—it was easy to do, as I'd been writing down his words all day. When he pretended to be a mother who wanted to talk it over with her husband first, I knew to remind her that they could try the knives for thirty days at no cost. "Why not get the knives now, try them out, and see what you think? If you and your husband decide you don't want them, no problem at all. I'll come pick them up myself and ship them back for you." I would steal Phil's techniques, including asking the role-playing customer to bring over the drawer that held the current household knives. Someone would pretend to carry over a drawer, and I'd talk about how the ghost knives had wooden handles that carried bacteria and wore down over time, while all Cutco products were guaranteed to last forever.

If I could have taken a test on being a salesman in that strip mall conference room, I would have aced it. But turned loose into real kitchens and living rooms, I couldn't replicate it. I knew what I was supposed to say during the demo, more or less down to the words. "Mr./Mrs. _____, since I just started, I don't want to miss any important details. I'm going to be reading a lot from my manual. Is that okay with you? Great. Well, Cutco is an awesome product and I'm excited to show it off. As I said over the phone, you don't have to buy anything but if you see something you like, you can get it today. You can buy sets or individual pieces and we have tons of wonderful accessories and gifts. One of the great things about Cutco is our interest-free, monthly investment options. So, if you get something today, you don't have to pay for it all at once. Cutco rocks so if you decide to get something today, you'll thank yourself for years to come! Thank you so much for taking the time to see my presentation—it really means a lot. . . . ."What I actually said: "Thanks for having me. Well, let me show you how these things cut." It was much harder to disregard the reality of someone's finances or criticize their current knives when I knew I wouldn't see the rush of joy in Phil's eyes as I gave the right answer. I could cut through the penny all right, but nobody pulled out their wallet as the blade sliced through Lincoln's eye. Selling knives may have been no less compromising than vacuuming floors, but it required more. You had to talk, cajole, risk offending. Even when I did stay more or less on script, that alone wasn't enough.

My demonstrations seldom lasted as long as they were supposed to. I waited to call Phil for my sales reports so he wouldn't know that.

~

We indeed got paid by the appointment, but while the appointments took a little under an hour (and less for me), we didn't get paid for travel time, or for the time we spent on the phone with Phil after each demo to workshop how it had gone. "Phoning = working" was said often in training, but we didn't get paid for setting up the appointments, either. The appointments also only counted if they were with someone who met the following criteria: married with a house and a full-time job. This was devastating news for Brad and I, as we'd planned on cleaning up with $12.50 demonstrations to all of our friends.

~

Since none of my friends met the appointment criteria, I scheduled with family members and other patient Mormons. I grabbed the ward directory out of the drawer at my parents' house and called people I hadn't spoken to in years. I read the script.

"Hi, Brother Childs, this is Michael Palmer. I'm doing well, thank you. How are you? That's great to hear. Well, the reason I'm calling is I just started a great, new job showing Cutco. As part of my training, I'm required to put on some initial training appointments. You don't have to buy anything, because I get paid just to show it. . . . "

"Is this the knives?" he asked.

". . . yes," I said.

"You can come by Saturday morning."

~

Phil loved to say "Touchdown!" on the phone after we sold a set, something I learned from Brad, who—although he made the jerkoff motion any time Phil turned his back—nevertheless was able to confirm that he'd scored multiple touchdowns. He didn't even have the Mormon phone tree to work with, but he'd sold multiple kitchen sets to family members. All I ever sold were the individual pieces of pity—a potato peeler here, an ice cream scoop there. If missionary work was anything like sales, I doubt I would have baptized a soul.

Of course, it was harder to close a sale in person than in practice, but Phil still seemed genuinely perplexed by how often I'd sold nothing at all. I never learned what his cut of our sales was, but he certainly acted invested. He always gave feedback. He usually asked first if I'd read the script, which was easy enough to lie about. Then he'd ask how it had gone at the end. As a way of wrapping up the presentation, we were supposed to ask the customer to review her address book and see if she could refer us to anyone to set up another demo. "Ask them if they know anyone who has kids, who likes to cook, who barbecues. . . ." We were supposed to clean up slowly so they could think of as many people as possible. I never did any of this. By the time a demo was over, I was more ready to leave than they were to show me the door. I lied about it at first, filling out the forms myself with some new Mormons. But eventually I ran out of names and had to tell Phil that I'd forgotten or been unable to ask for one reason or another.

"Come on, you know this!" he said to me once on the phone. And I knew what he was saying. Even I wasn't sure why I was so much worse outside of training. There was something holding me back, and it wasn't just that I didn't really want to do it. That was every job. Had I not recently trained myself to be a smiling call-center robot, in a place no one lasted, eventually becoming so proficient at logging surveys that I confused my supervisors? But at the call center, I felt I had no other option. Here, I knew I could always keep vacuuming. Without that desperation, I felt more comfortable acting like myself, and that did not help me sell knives because I did not believe like Phil believed. Phil could basically persuade me that the knives were a good product and we should sell them with pride, but he convinced me in the same way that Brad could convince me in a philosophical argument about the meaning of life. Sure, I might not have a great counter-argument ready to go, but I did not have the bone-level certainty that they did.

As my failures increased, my sparkling attitude dimmed. While I had never argued with Brad when he roasted Phil, I started dangling more carrots to get him going. To Brad, Phil was the embodiment of everything he despised: so slavishly devoted to profits that he would use the knives to cut out the heart of a puppy if it meant 1 percent more sales. As with everything else, my view of Phil was less certain. He was compelling enough that I would completely believe his intentions at 10:00 a.m., and swear to Brad he was the Antichrist by 10:00 p.m. I claimed that Phil's gleeful obsession with his job was what ruined work for the rest of us, while wondering if the shortcoming was actually mine and not his.

~

When I showed up to Brother Childs's house, he listened to the demonstration, bought an ice cream scoop, and then asked why they hadn't seen me in church for a while (half a decade).

"Well, it's just been a busy time," I said.

"I see. Well, we hope to see you back soon. You know, while you're here . . . there's some firewood on the lawn that I could really use moved into the shed. I'd be happy to pay an extra twenty dollars if you'd be willing to do that."

~

After the initial training, we mostly talked to Phil over the phone. But once every two weeks, our training group would rendezvous and share our experiences. I had almost always sold the least, and often became the workshop subject. These were the opposite of the earlier workshops we'd done, when I knew the answer to every question. This time, I would talk about a demo that hadn't resulted in a sale, and the others were invited to share methods they'd used for success in similar situations. (Remind them of the financing options, push harder for a commitment on the spot, pepper the presentation with constant reminders of what a big deal it was, and so on.)

~

Phil had shown up in a suit and a Porsche that first time, but after that he liked to run or bike to work. He wore Spandex exercise clothing. Unlike everything else he did, I don't think he wore the running apparel as a way to convey something about sales to us. I doubt the training encouraged that kind of clothing. I think that was Phil's individual passion.

He liked to start the morning by telling us there was nothing better than the runner's high. He would sometimes shake his head, puzzled by the large mugs of coffee he saw before him, while he said this.

I had always been suspicious of the runner's high, which sounded to me like a convenient story propagated by runners to get people to join their cult. But as usual, when Phil talked about it, I believed, at least for a moment, that I should take up running.

As he grew more comfortable in his clothing, so did Phil start to reveal his philosophical side to us, albeit always through a filter of sales.

"After the appointment is set, that's when the fun begins. And I just love it. If it doesn't make you happy, why do it?" he said one day. He claimed that the demos were so fun that he would have done them for free.

This is something I've heard from many people in many jobs over the years, and every time I hear it, I think of Phil. Who knows if he meant anything he was saying, as I tend to believe, or if he just felt that the line could convince us to stick around longer so he could profit off our sales, as was Brad's take. Regardless, when he said that, I conjured up the haunting image of Phil sitting alone at a table, scissors in hand, joker grin stretched across his unblemished face, a carpet of shredded pennies at his feet.

I heard what he was saying, but could never fully internalize it. In my heart, I had never done a job for anything other than money. I could talk myself into a job being less horrible or evil than other jobs—but only other jobs. Never in contrast to my non-job life. It wouldn't be accurate to say I envied Phil, but I wouldn't say I pitied him either. I just couldn't get where he was. I felt a mild sadness about my inability to relate, as I knew I would always have a job, whether I learned to love it or not.

I stopped taking Phil's calls toward the end of summer. I told Brad that it just wasn't in me to manipulate people like that, called the position more scam than job. That all might have been true, but even as I said it, I wished I felt it more strongly. I would have loved to deliver a passionate, sincerely-felt rant about Phil's vacuity. But the truth is, I didn't feel too good for the job; I just couldn't do it well, and I could survive without it. If I didn't have the vacuuming to fall back on, I would have tried harder.

Altogether, I made probably six hundred dollars, one hundred of which covered my own kit of knives. I never once heard Phil say, "Touchdown!" After a few more touchdowns of his own, Brad ran out of people to call, too. He found a telemarketing job with steadier hours.

~

For as hard as we worked to corner people into buying them, the products actually were good. I still have mine. The Spatula Spreader, in particular—with its flat, bendy body, and serrated edge—has been a major player over the years. When I see the knives, they remind me of my short-lived time as a salesman, when I still hoped that knowledge might be the only thing needed to fully buy or sell anything.

# Boyfriend

For me, beginnings are often more memorable than what comes after. Not to say better—just more memorable. The opening line of a gorgeous piece. The recognition of a previously unseen path. The first taste of coffee or the first sound of a wave crashing. Beginnings are made of the same material as smells. They create an obsession with tracking the concrete source of a feeling that can't be held.

~

Driving to Vegas, Anna wound through the canyoned corner of northwest Arizona at eighty miles an hour while looking for some kind of symbolic rock. I had a camcorder and was filming. During the famous descent into the Vegas lights, I turned the camera on her instead. She looked calm. . . .

~

We started dating by default, not knowing what else to do after sleeping together in the Astro van at the base of the mountain. I don't know the first time I called Anna my girlfriend. I called her "Honey" first.

I went from never having a girlfriend to being in a serious relationship, and what struck me was how easy it was. Church had taught me a lot about the "sacrifice and challenge" required to maintain a healthy marriage, but I now considered those lessons to be full of shit. Sure, I was afraid I was doing it wrong and, sure, I was afraid Anna would leave, but as for the actual day-to-day, what was so hard about it? We spent time together. Talked, cooked, read. There was nothing to it. I felt superior to other couples, who all struck me as dreary and pointless pairings who preferred spending time with their friends.

~

We were young and had nothing. It wouldn't quite be accurate to say we were poor. If one of us had gotten sick, our parents would have paid the hospital bills or died trying. We didn't have kids of our own to support. We had food and alcohol and sometimes a car. A mattress and box springs on the floor with her chinchilla in the corner. But the rest of the room was empty, save for each other and some books strewn over the carpet like birdseed.

∼

After the Greek gods in the mall told us to buy furniture, Anna and I watched a pirate show from the boardwalk. We absorbed the story's confusing conflict between the female and male pirates on the glassy sea. Then the conflict switched to dancing. We felt the warmth of the flames when one of the boats was destroyed for the second time that hour. It was not a good show. We loved it. That was our first trip together, five and a half hours south of home.

∼

Not every beginning telegraphs what's going to happen next. The first time I tasted coffee, I was in a McDonald's parking lot. I burned my tongue and my eyes watered with hatred. I poured a silo of sugar into the cup to tame it and swore off Satan's drink anew. I now drink it daily, and don't know a rival pleasure.

∼

Some crows left the tree as we approached, but the murder maintained the shell-shape of the tree, as if trying to recreate what they'd experienced.

∼

In Wendover, we ate at a faux-Paris restaurant with pinholes in the purple ceiling to approximate stars. She took a bath in the hotel and in the morning we wandered around the desert drinking Bud Light mixed with Clamato tallboys. I remember thinking I could have done that forever, if only I didn't have to go back to work.

∼

When it was too cold to walk home, I'd pick Anna up from her job at the restaurant. After a long shift, she would browse the radio until she found a song she knew and crank it up. She would scream the songs of whatever came out of the speakers, on whatever theme and in whatever tempo or tone, as long as she knew the words. She would howl until she burned the customer-service tone out of her voice.

≈

Anna and I spent one summer apart; not split up, just apart while she visited family in North Carolina. I waited for her at the airport next to a large family welcoming home a Mormon missionary. I was ecstatic to be there; I loved feeling warm in an airport while it was freezing outside, loved the returning missionary, loved the shiny, gilled, baggage carousel serpents. I wanted to move into the airport.

≈

There were times when we both worked our bullshit jobs so endlessly that stories of relaxation upset us. Our friends would tell us stories about getting high and watching movies, and we would despise them, failing to remember that the story had started as a sad one about unemployment and loneliness.

≈

We both knew the four who drowned in the cave, and up until that point we'd experienced no greater loss than lost religion. I'm glad we had each other then.

≈

It's also worth considering the beginning before the beginning, since this seems key to the beginning's kick. The unspoken hunger before the realized desire. The tingle of something unsaid, before Anna's name—on the page, on the screen—started to smell like raspberries.

≈

I have heard people describe relationships, particular the virginity-breakers, as "making them into a man," but this was not my experience exactly. I wasn't re-made. The person I became after that first time was already there. I did have a little more vision—a glimpse into a place beyond where my longing had been able to see to that point.

∽

That night at Utah Lake, the wind whipping in all directions. We'd walked down while the sun was out and during the walk it got too stormy to walk back. We hid in the rest area to get out of the wind and watched sheets of rain explode on the blacktop. Afterward it had a slick, licorice glow. It was too cold to fool around and we just stood there holding each other, breathing visible breath.

∽

Given the option, I would not recommend waiting until one's twenties to losing one's virginity. Outside of the realm of religion, there is nothing to be gained. But I'm glad I lost it when I lost it.

∽

The things I'm about to describe here I noticed because of Anna. She taught me how to pay attention. From her, I learned first how to recognize details. And then how to hunger for them.

∽

Say the whole thing was just a repetition of the beginning. I wouldn't mind that. But I'm not sure what it would look like.

∽

Probably love is a feeling that needn't be measured, scaled, explained, or maybe even described. And indeed the act of loving is quite dissimilar to the one of explaining. But I don't know how to account for things another way.

∽

I remembered the feeling years later when I unsuccessfully tried to seduce you in the hotel, knowing you were with someone else. *Oh yeah*, I thought. I've moved further along, learned to love in new ways in other realms that I will feel lucky I've experienced if I have time to reflect on my life before I die. But I still remember the initial mornings, the coffee percolating, a gray winter outside and us warm inside.

~

A habit I'm aware of but have been unable to break: I get starry-eyed and nostalgic when I feel I've done something whole-heartedly. As if the sweat and tears can pay for the indulgence.

Before I met Anna, the most serious relationship I'd had was making out with Christy in the park when I was fifteen. I spent our early days together in pure terror that it was all about to disintegrate. Eventually it did, but not for a while.

# Birdwatcher

By day I met my brother's mission friends from Ecuador and by night I confronted the birds.

In the day the sunlight dripped onto our skins and at night the darkness spilled into our ears and eyes. In the day my brother spoke Spanish and I tried to absorb it; at night we both spoke English, and sometimes he would forget how to pronounce words like "terminal." By day I ordered milk or orange soda and by night I mixed rum with my coke and I did it on the sly because my brother would have been offended. By day I was jealous of my brother and his familiarity with the country and the language. By night I was relieved that I would be going home soon. In the day we talked with Alberto about the birds. Besides managing the hotel, Alberto was into cockfighting. He was a mad geneticist of sorts and experimentally bred different birds together, hoping to come up with breeds that would be good fighters. At night Alberto was asleep and the birds were there without any explanation. In the day, Alberto told us that of all the birds, he was most amazed by the eagle chickens. According to him, they were what they sounded like: the result of an eagle bred with a chicken. Whatever they were, they were dark monstrosities with yellow eyes and they lingered on spindly bushes that sagged toward the ground under their weight. I never saw them fly, never even saw them walk around; they just sat on those bushes and made a horrible, non-avian sound, like a tired, old cat begging to come inside.

At night the birds were harder to spot, but you knew they were in the bushes somewhere. In the day Matt and I could watch the birds from a safe distance on the roof and they did not seem too intimidating; at night we had to use the side of the hotel to navigate through the thick darkness and then look at the porch light to know where we needed to go. In the day we paid fifty cents to ride in the back of a pickup truck out to some silent farms far from the city. My brother had baptized a family out there. At night we rode in the back of the same truck but didn't talk the whole way. In the day we had to decide if we wanted to head back early so we could get to the hotel before Alberto locked the front door and went to bed; at night we had to regret not getting there earlier and having to go around back and walk through the valley of birds.

At night, the bright yellow eyes of the eagle chickens floated in the darkness like crocodile eyes just above the water.

# The Archivists

MOURNING. *See* DEATH, DESPAIR, FASTING, FUNERALS, GNASHING OF
TEETH, GRAVES, GRIEF, SACKLOTH AND ASHES, SIGNS OF THE TIMES,
SOLEMEN ASSEMBLIES, SORROW, WEEPING. 1. Wholesome and proper
mourning—mourning based on sound gospel knowledge—is a profitable and
ennobling part of life. Men are commanded to fast, and pray,
and mourn: all these are essential parts of true worship.
—Bruce R. McConkie, *Mormon Doctrine.*

What's the schema for *no-longer-cheerleader?*
—Christine Marshall, *Match*

## 600 Feet into Granite Mountain, A Vault

The mountain is called granite but the rock is technically quartz
monzonite. It looks like granite, though—gray and strong and
eternal. The same rock was used to construct the Salt Lake Temple,
the spiky, rain-colored building in downtown Salt Lake. Inside the
mountain vault is a collection of dates, artifacts, histories, maps,
and names. Names of not just church members, but their ancestors,
possible converts, never-got-a-chances. The vault is said to hold the
largest collection of genealogical records in the world. Millions of
rolls of microfilm, digital media, diaries, maps. Records of all the
living and the dead and where they came from. All the names and
stories, sealed in rock where they can't be lost.

## 7-Eleven on State Street and 800 North

Home for the wedding, I could see the mountains the whole way,
but not full-on—in front of me, cars, clouds of birds, new housing
developments, and skinny young trees consumed my immediate vision.
Besides, I still knew the place in the same unthinking way I knew my
own breathing patterns. Not until I hit the red light waiting to cross
State Street, facing east, did I see them—and in that sight, the sensory
perceptions clicked on. I knew the view—the G on the mountain, the

peak of Timpanogos—and I felt for a moment that I was back in a place where everything had stayed the same. I imagined a parallel version of myself—skinnier, blue jeans and high tops—crossing State Street on foot as I'd done so many times before. I backed my car up and turned into the 7-Eleven, where I carefully read the nutritional content of soft drinks, buying time before going home.

## 1820, Spring of

According to the official version, this is the origin story: A fourteen-year-old boy, struggling to know which religion was true, walked into a grove of trees near his home and prayed about it. At first he was wrapped in unnatural daytime darkness—but a light shone down and two visages appeared. In the cartoon rendition I watched as a kid, young Joseph Smith had to lift his arm to shield his eyes from the light while he listened to the voice of God. *See also* **Vision, First.**

## Anderson, Brad

My best friend growing up, as well as the only non-Mormon I knew. On Sundays, he played Sega Genesis, drank Coke, and ate Double Stuf Oreos while the rest of us were at church. His mom was a defense attorney, and defended the Lafferty brothers in court. She died, of cancer, when Brad was fourteen. He had two much-older sisters who had already moved out by then. After his mom died, it was just his dad and him, and he was home alone all the time.

Worldliness-wise, he was always a few steps ahead of me, crossing things off his list before I'd had a chance to even imagine them. He did have a tendency to embellish the things he'd done—for the wide-eyed stares this inspired in me—but even accounting for that, he was ahead of me when it came to all of the eventual adolescent transgressions: sluffing class, shoplifting, drugs, tattoos, sex. Of course, he got a head start because he got to skip the big one: sluffing church. *See also* **Lafferty Brothers; Sluff.**

## As They Walked, Pioneer Children Sang

The Mormon pioneers arrived in Utah in 1847, and 150 years later, the youth of our ward were supposed to recreate a version of that trek with handcarts of our own. Mostly we pulled the handcarts from campsite to campsite, where food that had been hauled in by SUVs was waiting for us. In between campsites, we sang: *Pioneer children sang as they walked and walked / and walked and walked. They washed at streams and worked and played. / Sundays they camped and read and prayed. / Week after week, they sang as they walked and / walked and walked and walked and walked.*

### Attire of the Pioneers

We were encouraged to wear pioneer attire on the trek, but I either forgot about that or pretended I didn't know. I was wearing a Utah Jazz T-shirt and jeans. After everything was loaded into the Suburbans and pickups, Jacob Barney asked me if I would offer the prayer on the front lawn of the church before we departed for the mountains. I was asked to participate in things like that often—a way of including me when I never volunteered for anything. What did I pray about? To myself: that the trek would end early, as with the miraculous scouting trip shortened due to weather two winters ago. Aloud: that we would return home safely.

### Awfulness

This is the word my mother uses to account for any unpleasant parts of a story—whether personal anecdote or family history. She can use it to refer to large-scale events—divorces, disappearances, children born out of wedlock, drownings; or small-scale ones—disobedience, delinquency, crass language, popular music. *See also* **Notes on My Family's Pioneer Stories.**

### Backslide

Refers to the process of slipping ever so slightly out of good standing in the church—perhaps due to an overindulgence in worldly habits such as drinking, swearing, light blasphemy, or simply not going to church. Sometimes the slide is temporary, and other times it spirals to permanent separation. *See also* **Excommunication; Exile.**

## Beliefs

Later on, when people asked me why I stopped going to church as a teenager, I said it was because going to church was boring, and I wanted to sin. I wanted tattoos, premarital sex, alcohol, drugs. While I did experience most of those perks eventually, only the first part—not attending church—was immediate. Indeed, I was proudly straight edge; I dyed my hair black and told people how fucked up it was that they couldn't enjoy themselves without clouding their minds with substances, words I had stolen from my friend Karen's boyfriend Jacob, who was several years older than we were, loved the words "positive" and "stoked," had one full sleeve of tattoos and knew how to fight. I started to attend hardcore shows with him and Karen. He taught me that it was called a "show," not a "concert." The kids at the shows wore hoodies that said "I WOULD DIE TONIGHT FOR MY BELIEFS." I traded one group of certain white people for another. *See also* **X**.

## Blessing

My father would give me and my three siblings a blessing in our living room to correspond with any life change—from an illness to a summer camp to the first day of school. He would rub consecrated oil into his palms, place his hands on our heads, and bless us. Warm calloused hands and the smell of BRUT and the sight of our brown carpet when I opened my eyes during his prayer. In a standard blessing, he would ask Heavenly Father that we be kind, and confident, and appreciate our God-given talents. *See also* **Santaquin**.

## Book of Mormon

Subtitle: Another Testament of Jesus Christ. BoM for short. Continues the stories from the Bible, on the American continent. It's been called the "Mormon Bible," but Mormons do not call it this, as they also believe in the Bible Bible. Mark Twain called it "chloroform in print." Some historians have analyzed the language patterns to conclude that it was a contemporary text and not an ancient translation. Others have read it as a collage—Smith's jury-rigging of various theological ideas in the air during his time.

Mormons encourage potential converts to read the book, and then ask about its truth in prayer. Say you do so and get an answer in the affirmative. Whatever its merits as a page-turner, I'm not sure the above criticisms are significant at that point. Wherever Smith's inspiration came from, how can you plagiarize the word of God? *See also* **Golden Plates.**

## Center of the Center of Mormondom

The headquarters of the LDS Church are in Salt Lake City, but the true heart of Mormonism is about forty miles south of there, in Utah County, my home region. The mountains there are taller, and closer to the city than they are in Salt Lake; they're visible from nearly everywhere, even if you have to lift your eyes from a billboard advertising a gun show to see them. The mountains loom over the region, their peaks mimicked by the white church steeples, all pointing up.

My family attended church every week—all three hours. If we were out of town, we would find the nearest ward and attend there. My upbringing was one of board games and folding chairs and punch mixed with Sprite. I attended BYU football games with my uncle and couldn't keep track of my cousins. On Saturdays, our family volunteered to help clean the church. On Wednesdays, there were youth activities—camping or broom hockey or basketball. I was never alone.

## Chelsea Ford

Utah County through and through, Chelsea married my younger brother Matt in 2012. As a kid, she won an award for a photo-essay titled "If Cats Could Talk." As an adult, she rescues animals and fosters cats in her home—as many as seven at a time. The most cross thing I ever heard her say was, "You are making me swear in my head."

She and my brother invited me to come home for their wedding after I hadn't been in Utah for what had only been two years but felt like a distance that would be impossible to walk back, in part because my purpose in Utah had dried up. But this was the first time

I had a job to do if I returned. I said yes. *See also* **7-Eleven on State Street and 800 North; Matthew; Reception.**

## Cultural Hall

Every Mormon church has one: a large, versatile reception space for events. Ours had basketball hoops, a piano, and a stage. It was also connected to a kitchen. We set up rows of metal folding chairs for meetings. For activities, we might fill the space with cheap plastic pools so we could bob for apples, or set up a cakewalk with the same song playing on repeat for hours: *And I miss you / Like the deserts miss the rain.* Shirtless basketball games with acne-ridden shoulders. Trick shots from the stage. The echoes of the basketball dribbling.

## Colorado, East of

My father often mentioned that he had never been east of Colorado. He didn't mention it with shame or pride, it was just a fact about his life, delivered in a similar tone as the year of his birth (1948). Then one year my parents saved their money so that we could fly as a family to New York and drive back, tracing the route of the early Mormon pioneers but in a rented minivan. This was in 1998, one year after our ward's pioneer trek in the mountains. I was fourteen.

## Distance to Texas

a) I told my parents Texas wasn't really that far away when I moved, but it was. Anywhere else would have been. I didn't even return for holidays. I would let people in Texas think I was going home so that they wouldn't feel bad and invite me to anything. And then I'd spend Thanksgiving or Christmas walking around the desolate city, the downtown Lubbock stoplights flashing yellow.

b) It took physically leaving the state for me to feel that I had fully left the church, and even then the loss would sometimes rush back to me: meeting Mormons in Lubbock and remembering the community that would have been built-in for me there had I stayed in the church; trying to form a basketball league but being incapable of the required organization. And, of course, remembering every Sunday that I had no place to be.

## Downtown Salt Lake City

The shows would be at Brick's or DV8, usually. We'd take the 600 South exit and eat at Sage's or Evergreen, vegan restaurants, beforehand. Outside the venue, black-hoodied youth, aged anywhere from fifteen to thirty-five, would appear out of nowhere by the hundreds. I hardly ever saw them outside of that context and was stunned by their numbers. What they called dancing looked like a mosh pit full of karate school dropouts. Blades of white arms flying everywhere, collisions, blood on the floor. It was exhilarating to watch, but I couldn't move like that. The few times I went in the pit, I would just jerk my fist forward three times, like an alien trying to impersonate a fan at a sporting event, as I moved from one side to the other. Then back to the margins to watch. *See also* **X**.

## Dreams

a) As a child born to parents with big debt and a farm of rocks, Joseph Smith's big dream was to avoid the tedious, solitary work of the plow. When he was young, he sought treasure in the countryside.

b) A famous dream of Lehi's, from the Book of Mormon: Lehi glimpses the Tree of Life. Again, my visual for this comes from the cartoon in which the fruit on the tree glows the color of faeries. Surrounding the tree is a thick mist of darkness. The only way to get to the tree is to take hold of an iron rod and follow it as a guide. Lehi approaches the tree and partakes of the fruit, and invites his family to do so also. His wife and two of their four sons follow him, but the other sons do not. They are eventually spotted in a "great and spacious building" with the other wanderers, mocking those eating the fruit below.

c) I had this dream two nights ago. I was at a Utah Jazz game, before the arena renovation, when the seats were still green. Performers on stilts interrupted the game in the first quarter and I started to walk around the arena. I saw my scoutmaster and my church ball coach and Mitt Romney and other Mormon authority figures. Outside a concession stand, my father said, "I pray that everything is going SUPER well," words that look sarcastic when written but that is how he talks. I returned to my seat to find the game had resumed. David

Stockton, John Stockton's son and the starting point guard in this reality, dove out of bounds for a loose ball.

## Excitement

a) "Excitement has become almost the essence of my life," Smith said in a sermon in 1843. "When that dies away I feel almost lost." The comment was said somewhat in jest, alluding to the "excitement" of having to dodge attacks, both on his character and his life. Whatever else it might have been—and there are definitely other words that could describe it—his life was exciting. He hid from the law, had dozens of wives, and succeeded in avoiding farm life.

b) To the extent that I became rebellious after I stopped going to church, it was apparent even at the time how tepid that rebellion was. Nevertheless, every activity that was different from what I was supposed to be doing and had always done carried with it a charge of excitement. At night, Brad and I jumped the fence of the community pool, stole the wooden shark that measured whether or not you were tall enough to ride the waterslide, threw it over the fence, and stuffed it into his car—its blue-green measuring fin pointing out the window. We sluffed class and shoplifted black hair dye from beauty salons. I saw the text *GRAFFITI LOVES YOU* painted on a train, then decided to copy that message. I bought some paint and wrote the same thing on a white fence on our street. The fence was vinyl and the text bled into a drippy, Halloween font. It was there for three days and then painted over. "That wasn't you, was it?" my mom asked as we drove past it one day. "I think I deserve a little more credit than that," I said. *See also* **Sluff; Theft.**

## Excommunication

a) Sometimes members of the church are excommunicated for failing to live up to those "worthiness standards" required for church membership. But even in Joseph Smith's time, excommunication tended to happen not so much to the unworthy as to those who were not only critical of certain doctrine, but had a loud enough voice for people to notice their criticism. A recent example of a prominent excommunication: Kate Kelly, founder of Ordain Women, argued that women should have the priesthood, and was exed.

b) I have known ex-Mormons who wear their excommunication as a badge of honor; but for reasons I can't quite figure out, and even though I will never go back to church, I still dread that final severing. It seems too final a detachment, leaving me with nowhere to claim as home. *See also* **Exile; Part-Member; Post-Mormon; Recovering Mormon.**

## Exile

a) The early Mormons left Ohio because of dissension within their own community. They were driven out of Missouri because they were gaining too much political power. Out of Illinois because Smith destroyed a printing press, and the non-Mormons of the state, sensing the rise of theocratic power around them, threw him into jail where he was murdered.

b) It was my choice to go to Texas. But I did feel I had to leave Utah.

## Facing Zion

That summer of 1997, pioneer stories were the rage. The prevailing story from my own family was about "wee granny," who tried to make the trip west in her seventies. Somewhere along the way, her health faltered, and she didn't make it. As the story goes, before she died, someone asked what message she wanted relayed to her family. "Tell them I died facing Zion," she said. *See also* **Notes on My Family's Pioneer Stories; Zion.**

## Faith

a) Early on, long before Smith was an established prophet, there's a story about a young man, Newel Knight, being "afflicted with Satan" and rolling around on the floor. A dozen people crowded into the room, unsure what to do. They looked to Smith, and he realized that he was expected to act. With whatever degree of conviction, he reached out and seized Knight's hand. "Almost immediately he spoke to me," Joseph wrote in his autobiography, "and with great earnestness requested me to cast the devil out of him, saying that he knew he was in him, and that he also knew that I could cast him out." The convulsions ceased. *See also* **Dreams**.

b) According to my mom, faith is the feeling that you are where God wants you to be, doing what He wants you to be doing. She understood the feeling immediately when she was hit with a warm calmness while attending church as a kid.

c) I used to wonder if such certainty was looking for me, too, but finding my heart closed. To this day, I don't understand faith, which is not the same as not understanding how someone could possibly have faith. I mean, I don't understand what faith means. In the Smith story above, faith seems to be a kind of manic confidence, whereas for my mom it was a feeling of peace. I had a professor who described faith as "the substance of things hoped for." For my part, I remember a time when I was certain that the church was true, but I think the complexity of faith is maintaining that kind of belief once you've learned to doubt.

d) Then again, what if it isn't so hard to understand? As many do, I think about all of my dreams ending in failure, the world drying up, the air turning to poison. And I know I'm going to die. And yet every day I expect the sun. I try to buy as much time as I can.

## Family Home Evening

Mormon families devote one night a week to family time that is meant to be educational and fun. In my family, we would start by singing a hymn, and then someone would say a prayer. This would be followed by a lesson or activity of some kind—perhaps a brief lesson about Christ's salvation, or a plan to develop substitution swear words so we wouldn't use the real ones. (My father's choice—the only one that lasted—was "argh," like a pirate but without the pirate accent.) Once, when I was in charge of the lesson, I gave everyone a Tootsie Roll for promising to be righteous. I'm not saying all Mormon theology is comparable, that's just the kind of thing I came up with when I had to plan the lesson myself. Thus, my respect for the Book of Mormon.

## Golden Plates

Smith used a shovel to unearth the plates from a hill in the New York countryside. In order to translate the ancient language, Smith used a seer stone that he placed into a hat. He would peer into the hat, and in the darkness, a spiritual light would shine.

Before that, Smith went from congregation to congregation trying to determine which church was true. I heard this story many times, including from our tour guide when we visited the Sacred Grove in upstate New York. Noting my age, similar to Smith's at that time, she looked at me and said, "Imagine being in his shoes, with no awareness of the Truth we know today. What would you do?" *See also* **Book of Mormon; Excitement.**

**Goodly Parents**

a) In the Book of Mormon, Nephi's first statement is a tribute to his parents. The text reads: "I, Nephi, having been born of goodly parents, therefore I was taught somewhat in all the learning of my father." *See also* **Blessing; Dreams.**

b) My parents married late for Mormons. My dad was thirty-three; my mom, twenty-six. He proposed to her on Mount Timpanogos. They had both served missions by then: my dad in California, and my mom in Holland. Together, they had four kids: my sisters Mindi and Amanda, myself, and Matthew. My dad is an enthusiastic man, in particular with regard to Mormon subjects, to the degree that his sincerity would sometimes make me cringe as a kid. When friends would come over, he would greet us by saying, "There's two dudes!" My mother is only slightly less sincere. She enjoys a good prank, though not all kinds. In her words, "I do not care for pranks that destroy property or that are unkind or demeaning. I love the creative kind that cause us to all laugh together." For example: unloading excess zucchini onto unsuspecting neighbors in increasingly creative ways. She built a beautiful backyard featuring fruit trees, a bright green lawn, a giant willow tree, burning bushes, lilacs, and a garden. She likes to sit back there and feed the gray jays peanuts by hand.

**Great Salt Lake**

I always took a little bit of pride that it was large enough to show up on maps of America, distinguishing Utah from the other western states, all right angles and blankness. But aside from that, we were taught to avoid the lake. Told that it smelled sulfuric; that it was overrun with brine flies; that swimming there would be absurd. Nobody talked about the light transforming to redness in the water, or the way the slow water whispered, as if you could hear the salt breathing.

## Heavens

a) Mormon heaven breaks down into three tiers. Ranked from best to worst, there are the Celestial, Terrestrial, and Telestial Kingdoms. Jesus Christ and righteous people reside in the Celestial Kingdom. The major drawback of the lesser kingdoms—which are still pretty nice, when contrasted with most hells—is that you are barred from the company of Christ and the righteous souls for eternity. This is what my mom was talking about when, after I stopped going to church, she told me, "You are making choices with eternal consequences based on how you feel right now. As a teenager!"

b) There's the brightly dressed twin of existential despair, panic not over the abyss but the incomprehensible endless dread of something going on forever, every action taken, every joke made, every prophecy fulfilled, everything understood.

## House, Empty

With three siblings, two parents, and a constant churn of mandatory wholesome activity, I had never really been alone—until I stopped going to church and had the house to myself during that three-hour block. Along with being prime masturbation hours, this space allowed permission to be as loud or quiet as possible. To blast my music or to climb on the roof and watch the clouds pass in front of the mountains. Or to go for a walk, which was comparably thrilling since the whole neighborhood had emptied out in the same way.

## Ice Cream

It is an exaggeration to say that Mormons are obsessed with ice cream. But not much of one. When I was a kid and would go to work with my father—a real estate agent-handyman hybrid who was often on call to repair things—he would always conclude work with a trip to the Dairy Queen drive-thru where he ordered a chocolate-coated vanilla ice cream cone. His truck didn't have power steering so he would hand me his cone while he cranked the wheel to the right to get back on State Street headed toward home.

I like ice cream okay, but not like my father. I once asked my mom why Mormons loved ice cream so much, and she said, "It's delicious, so what's the harm?" "Cholesterol, blood pressure, obesity. . . ." "Yeah, well," she said. "It still beats alcohol."

## Infant in the Water

On the pioneer trek, our "families" were challenged to retrieve something that was floating in the middle of a lake on a raft. I couldn't tell what it was at first, but someone said, "It's a baby!" Just a plastic one. My team won this prize by fashioning some branches together with tape and twine and wading out just far enough to reach the baby. We must have raked its face a dozen times but we guided it in. I say "we" loosely, as I stood on the shore and pretended to be involved, but didn't really do anything. Our prize was a cantaloupe.

I'd like to reflect for a moment on this exercise, as I have thought of it often over the years. Say a baby really went missing from the wagon train. How did it get on that raft? Is the implication that another pioneer would have placed it there? That the baby fashioned the raft in order to escape? I understand now that these things are often rigged up on the spot, and our leaders were just trying to come up with a spur-of-the-moment activity. But this one led to the lasting, horrifying image of an infant cut off from the pack, drifting alone on the water. *See also* **As They Walked, Pioneer Children Sang; Water.**

## Jack Mormon

a) A sympathetic non-Mormon living among Mormons. *See also* **Backslide.**

b) A Mormon who is selectively observant. Basically, a backslider without the guilt. A Mormon at peace with her faith as well as her chosen desires of the world.

## John Riel

As a teenager, he had a mohawk and stopped going to church around the same time I did. But later in life, he became religious again—as a member of something called "the Rock Church." The last time I hung out with him, we went to Del Taco and decided to drive around like we had during high school. Without any kind of heads up, he parked in front of a Christian bookstore and asked if it was cool if we went in for a minute. *Veggie Tales* was playing on televisions throughout the store. He walked to the books about the historical and architectural backing of the Bible. "You know why Mormons don't have books with this kind of proof? Because there is none." I told him to calm down and said I didn't care, but I was seething on the ride home. Some of that old tribalism rushed through me, including judgment on Jeff for trading his membership in to be part of something called the fucking Rock Church. "Just be Mormon, you coward," I remember thinking but not saying.

## Journal of the American Family Association

Once all theological arguments had led to stalemates, my parents and I started to argue about politics. I practically screamed at them when I read about the timeline of the civil rights movement, when I'd always been told that the church had to wait "until the world was ready" to give black men the priesthood. 1978. My parents were also subscribers to the weekly journal sent out by the American Family Association, an evangelical group based out of Mississippi. The journal told the reader what to avoid and who to vote for, providing context-free clues about a television show's filth so you'd know not to watch it. I recall a feature story titled "Something Was Missing" about a woman who had previously been in a relationship with another woman. I couldn't abide a word of it; the writers seemed incapable of feeling joy unless imagining heathen orphans burning in hell.

And they were not fans of Mormons either. This was a point I tried to make repeatedly, but my parents felt that it was crucial to align with all aspects of American Christianity, since so many people still didn't know Mormons even believed in Christ. Indeed,

Mormons had been barred from attending an evangelical convention in Arizona because they weren't considered to be real Christians. But I could not convince my parents to shun the alliance in turn. *See also* **Unremitting Questions Everyone, Including Me, Is Sick Of.**

## Kirtland Temple

The first constructed Mormon temple. A relatively small, white building; the early converts crushed their china and used it to make the exterior of the temple sparkle in the sun. Unlike the temple in Nauvoo, it wasn't burned after the Mormons left, and still stands in Ohio. However, it is not owned by the LDS Church, but rather the Community of Christ (previously called the Reorganized Church of Jesus Christ of Latter-day Saints), which was started by Joseph Smith's son. After we visited the temple, my mother said, "Well, you can tell it's not run by us," not only because just anyone off the street could go inside and tour the building, but because the tour guide was wearing a tank top and shorts.

## Korihor

A character from the Book of Mormon who claimed that Christ would never come. Korihor was a kind of reverse missionary; he attempted to dissuade the people of Ammon of their beliefs, but they threw him out. Later he was imprisoned in Gideon for preaching atheism. He got into an argument with Alma, the chief judge and governor of the region. Alma said that the existence of God was everywhere, but Korihor demanded to be shown proof, in the form of a sign. Immediately he was struck deaf and mute. He later claimed the devil deceived him into thinking there was no God, and begged forgiveness. But Alma cast him out. He became a beggar and was later trampled to death by the Zoramites. *See also* **Excommunication.**

## Lafferty Brothers

On Pioneer Day in 1984, Ron and Dan Lafferty broke into Brenda Wright Lafferty's house in American Fork and used knives to murder her along with her infant daughter Erica. They claimed to have received a prophecy directing them to kill the women. Brenda was married to their youngest brother, Allen, and she had criticized the self-proclaimed seer status of Ron and Dan, refusing to let Allen join what they called the School of the Prophets. The story is chronicled in detail in Jon Krakauer's *Under the Banner of Heaven.*

They were caught in a buffet line in Reno. Both were sentenced to life in prison. In 1991, a federal appeals court overturned Ron's first conviction, saying that the judge had used the wrong standard of determining mental competency. He was re-tried in 1996, and one of his defense attorneys was Brad's mom, Linda Anderson. When she was diagnosed with cancer two years later, Ron said it was because she had tried to put a curse on him but he had deflected the curse back to her. Ron was convicted again and sentenced to die. As of this writing, through a series of appeals, he's still alive on death row. *See also* **Anderson, Brad.**

## Laman and Lemuel

In the Book of Mormon, the prophet Lehi had four sons. In order of birth, their names were Laman, Lemuel, Sam, and Nephi. Lehi had a revelation that Jerusalem was going to be destroyed, but nobody in the city would listen to him. When the destruction was nigh, he told his family they needed to leave. Laman and Lemuel griped about this pretty much the whole way, as they had left their homes and possessions in order to wander around in the desert. Their complaints continue throughout the Book of Mormon. Constantly Laman and Lemuel rebel against Nephi, the most righteous brother, only to be smitten by God for being such doubting fools. But they never learn their lesson, and eventually, after reaching America, they split off for good. The descendants of Laman and Lemuel came to be called Lamanites in the Book of Mormon; the descendants of Nephi and Sam the Nephites. And, of course, the Lamanites were cursed with dark skin for their sinful deviance.

To me as a kid, Laman and Lemuel were endlessly frustrating; constantly given tangible proof that God not only existed, but wanted them to perform a specific task, they nevertheless balked at it every time. I found them much more sympathetic characters when I reached adulthood. *See also* **Goodly Parents.**

## Light and Sound

At school, those of my friends who still went to church regularly no longer understood who I was or what I was doing. Or anyway, I projected that they felt that way, and drifted away from them. I fell in with Brad's friends, a group of students who came to school—if they came at all—mainly to snort Lortabs in the spotlight booth during Light and Sound class. I pretended to be put off by this and far above these actions, but that was in part because I had made being straight edge a core part of my identity before realizing I had access to drugs. *See also* **Beliefs; X.**

## Marriage, Eternal

a) A ritual performed in the temple which extends marriage into an everlasting bond. *See also* **Temple Recommend.**

b) Matt and Chelsea's reception was in my parents' backyard, but the actual ceremony took place in the Manti temple. Only those with a temple recommend were allowed inside. I didn't have one, so I waited in the visitor's center, where a short film about the construction of the temple played. The only other people in there were children, and one adult woman trying to keep them from choking on something or escaping. The movie was about twenty-five minutes long. After it was over, I walked around the temple. The sky was purple and the grounds were a vivid, almost unnatural green. I watched the swarms of bridesmaids take photos on the hill leading up to the temple for a while, then walked back into the visitor's center and watched the movie again, waiting for the ceremony to wrap up.

## Matthew

My younger, ultimately much more righteous brother. There was a blink of time when it looked like there was a chance he would backslide his way out of the church as well. He was prone to mindless destruction—hurling bricks through the windows of abandoned properties, and some light swearing. But he shaped up, served a mission in Ecuador, got a degree from BYU, and married Chelsea.

His mission, in particular, transformed him. He came back skinny, and confident. He took up cooking and started organizing excursions to Salt Lake to hear famous organists play. *See also* **Backslide; Chelsea Ford.**

### Mormon Country

A book written by Wallace Stegner, who said he wrote it "out of sheer homesickness for the west." In the book, Stegner writes: "The Mormons have never been an imaginative people; they never noticed much about the land they settled except that the sagebrush growth was sturdy or thin. In all that country you seldom find a house built to take advantage of the view, though the view is likely to be something tremendous." *See also* **Zion.**

### Moroni

The golden figure atop most Mormon temples. This is the angel who appeared one night, out of the pre-electricity darkness, and revealed to Smith where the golden plates were buried.

That was in 1823, three years after Smith met God. The delay in action is not really accounted for. The skeptical interpretation of the timeline is that Smith's account of the First Vision was a way of mythologizing his own past after the fact. But I prefer to think of the fourteen-year-old boy who, after glimpsing the radiance of God in upstate New York through his peripheral vision, did not really know what to do with that experience except go home and see what happened next. *See also* **1820, Spring of; Golden Plates.**

### Nauvoo

The city the Mormons built on the edge of the Mississippi River in Illinois. When my family stopped there, we made bricks and watched a blacksmith hammer us each a metal ring. We danced under starlight. Actually, I didn't. I waited by the car and listened to the far-off voices.

### No Job

a) I left Utah for good when I was twenty-five. I had an empty month between the time my lease in Salt Lake expired and the time I was supposed to be in Texas, during which time I moved back home. From my parents' basement, time moved in both directions. I would be trying to visualize what Texas might look like while vivid childhood memories reappeared to me.

b) It was hard to sleep there, and often I didn't. I was unemployed with nothing to do until July was over. At night, I would drive all over the state. My blue Chevy Celebrity sped into the purple night and away from city lights. I doubted my choice to leave the state, doubt similar to the feeling I had experienced years earlier when I had chosen—in my mother's words—to "reject the light of the Savior." I thought there was a chance I wouldn't see much of it ever again—or see it only in passing—no time to see the salt flats glowing under the moon, or the pink light behind the mountains at dawn.

c) Leaving the church meant stopping all of the other activities, too (except basketball). Other than school, my calendar was completely cleared. It was like getting fired, except I didn't have to find a new job.

## No Water

Our handcart company had to accommodate everyone, which meant our pace was incredibly slow. One day on the trek, a group decided to forge ahead and set up camp early. I ended up among them, preferring a faster, less musical pace. We moved quickly, and my legs were used to long strides on mountain slopes. But I drank my water too fast and didn't have a backup. I went without for most of the day, eventually asking Spencer if I could drink some of his. He said he was sorry, but he was almost out and needed it. By the time we made it to camp, I was nearly hallucinating from thirst. I had a filtering device that I used to get water straight out of a nearby stream. I drank as much as I could and fell asleep on the bank. Brother Evans found me later, mosquito bites all over, and said, "Are you having a good time?" I said, "Oh, yes. I must've gotten tired." *See also* **Water**.

## Notes on My Family's Pioneer Stories

The stories are designed for one takeaway only—the certainty that, with the help of our ancestors, we're on the right path, doing the right thing. Despite this insistence, not all characters or details stay where they're supposed to. Cousins adopted without explanation.

People vanishing for years then reappearing. A bear chained up at Utah Lake that the kids would taunt for entertainment.

## Oh, My Heck

"Oh, my gosh" is typically used to avoid taking the Lord's name in vain, but "oh my heck" is my personal favorite euphemism. The closest translation nationally is probably something like, "Oh, for hell's sake." Also in this category is one I've mainly heard my mom say: "Hecka good/proud." As in, "The way the Cougars played on Saturday made us hecka proud."

## Orchards

The Apple Grove housing developments are there now, but I grew up next to apple orchards, which I walked through to get to school. The clean scent of apples and heat in the summer. The prospect of seeing animals and the myth of the orchard owner prowling with a shotgun full of salt. The darkness the orchards provided when I wanted to scare myself at night. The white peaks of the mountains through the green leaves.

## Orientation

In Utah County, you always know which direction you're heading because the mountains are always to the east. When I moved to Texas, I tried to re-learn how to navigate. I never really did learn; I just got used to the town and where things were.

## Osmond, Marie

Singer, actress, writer, and TV show host, she is (along with her brother Donnie) one of the most famous Mormons, and one of my personal favorites. She wrote a book called *Marie Osmond's Guide to Beauty, Health, and Style*, which includes subtitles such as "Marie's Special Hints for Sewing Savvy," "Your Feet Need Some Attention, Too," and "Marie's Maxims." Sample maxim: "Life has to be balanced, like the four legs of a chair . . . or else."

After her father died, she said the Bible encouraged her to try out for a reality TV program involving dancing. She told the story of randomly opening to a passage from Ecclesiastes. "It said, 'There's a time to mourn and a time to dance.' And I felt like it was almost from my dad saying, 'This is your time to dance.'"

## Outer Darkness

A region totally removed from the light and glory of God. It is meant primarily for Satan and his followers in the pre-existence, who as a result of their betrayal were never given bodies here on earth and thus cannot be baptized or saved. But in addition to the sealed fate of those spirits, it's taught that there will be a few who lived and had bodies who end up there, silent souls floating through the abyss, watching the light. Nobody knows who. *See also* **Excommunication; Exile; Heavens.**

## Part-Member

An adjective—e.g., "My mom is Mormon, but my dad isn't, so we are a part-member family"—that sometimes feels like a noun.

## Pioneer Day

A state holiday in Utah on July 24. It commemorates the day the Mormon pioneers first entered Utah. The celebration has also been co-opted by the secular as "pie-and-beer day." One year, *The Daily Herald* published a national editorial arguing that Mormons care much more about Pioneer Day than the Fourth of July. My older sister Mindi, fifteen at the time, seething from the patriotic slight, wrote an indignant response detailing Provo's Fourth of July festivities. It was published in the *Herald*'s letters to the editor. *See also* **As They Walked, Pioneer Children Sang.**

## Poplar Trees

Wherever Mormons went, they planted poplar trees because they grow tall quickly. Long strands line ditches and streets, and act as boundaries between fields and farms. My mom planted them on the west side of our house.

Of these trees, Wallace Stegner said, "If the Heavenward aspirations of medieval Christianity found their expression in cathedrals and spires, the more mundane aspirations of the Latter-day Saints may just as readily be discovered in the widespread plantings of Mormon trees. They look Heavenward, but their roots are in earth. The Mormon looked toward Heaven, but his Heaven was a Heaven on earth and he would inherit bliss in the flesh." *See also* **Excitement; Promised Land; Zion.**

## Post-Mormon

Growing up, I felt defined by no category as closely as Mormon—not gender, race, class. Of course, I'm a white man with the luxury of ignoring those categories. Still, I thought in terms of Mormon and non-Mormon first.

Some of my friends who don't go to church anymore think of themselves as post-Mormon, but I am not quite there. For me, there is no graduation, no clean "post." No easy return, either.

## Promised Land

Initially, Smith said the Promised Land would stretch from Ohio all the way to the Pacific. Where the Mormons officially ended up was in the valleys of the Wasatch Mountains, though Smith never got that far. He did send some scouts out west before his death, instructing them to "hunt out a good location, where we can remove to after the temple is completed, and where we can build a city in a day, and have a government of our own, get up into the mountains, where the devil cannot dig us out, and live in a healthful climate, where we can live as old as we have a mind to." *See also* **Zion.**

## Qualification for Statehood

Mormons practiced polygamy (or "plural marriage") in the nineteenth century. There is a little uncertainty about how many wives Joseph Smith himself had, and the church has only recently been open about this information. But he had approximately forty wives, aged from fifteen to fifty-six.

Polygamy was officially discontinued in 1890, partially because the practice of polygamy was being held against Utah in its request to be granted statehood.

Some sects, such as the Fundamentalist Church of Jesus Christ of Latter-Day Saints, still practice polygamy, and I have seen their members a few times at places such as the St. George Costco—or at least I made that assumption based on their anachronistic clothing and hairstyles. Before the FLDS leader Warren Jeffs fled to Texas, and then got arrested, I drove through Colorado City once, which is where a large polygamist community used to be. Not one person was outside. No one seemed to follow me, either. It was as if they'd already gone. There was nothing to see. It probably looks the same now that they've departed.

## Reception

I helped to string up the lights and prepare the tables, showed people how to release Chinese lanterns into the sky above our neighborhood, and directed people to smear Oreos and other crap all over their car before they left. I distracted Uncle Gaylen when he said the Chinese lanterns were going to burn down the neighborhood. I positioned romantic photos of the couple on a table and then had someone with a better eye check my work. I stayed busy to avoid talking to relatives I hadn't seen in years. *Don't panic*, I told myself. The yard was filled with the scent of lilacs. Of course, there was no booze.

Everyone I'd ever seen throughout my childhood was there, one after another, a line of modest dresses and wide ties stretching from the backyard all the way into the street in front of our house. I'd only been out of Utah for two years, but I hadn't been to church in over a decade. Some of them didn't recognize me, though others did right away. I tried to explain where I'd been. *See also* **Distance to Texas.**

## Recovering Mormon

When I lived in Salt Lake City during graduate school, this is what my neighbor called himself. I once asked him if he thought he would ever be fully recovered. He thought for a while and said, "Honestly, we need our own AA." *See also* **Part-Member; Post-Mormon.**

## Reunion, Ten Years After High School

By sheer coincidence, my high school reunion was the same night as

Matt and Chelsea's wedding reception. I thought about going, but bailed. One reunion with that era was enough. Nevertheless, out of old teenage habit, I lied to my parents and told them I was going and wouldn't be back until late. When I first got back to Utah, I felt that nothing had changed; but that was mostly based on the view of the mountains. In reality, the area was exploding. I had to go much farther out for pitch darkness, and there were new developments everywhere. I drove up Provo Canyon, and wound up the mountain to the viewpoint we used to drive to in high school. I parked and looked out at the valley. From that perspective, it wasn't so different. Sparks of light for miles. The dark spot of the lake.

### Sad-Sack E-mail from My Mom, Two Months into My Time in Texas

"Tonight, Matt and Amanda volunteered to do dinner. Then we watched old home movies. Those really were the good old days, before the awfulness started. I'm glad we preserved the movies. Someday maybe I can get it on to DVD, but then they'll probably update the technology to something else." *See also* **Awfulness**.

### Sluff

I've never heard this word spoken out of Utah. It might be a derivative of "slough," which can mean a state of moral degradation or spiritual dejection. But in Utah it means to skip something, such as class or church, e.g., "Should we go to seminary or should we sluff?"

### Santaquin

When I was on the road to Texas, my father called me and said he'd wanted to give me a blessing before I'd left the house, but had been too afraid to ask because of the many church-related fights we'd had over the years. But he asked if I would turn around so he could give me a blessing.

I was only to Santaquin by then, about twenty-five minutes out. I said, "Oh. Dad, I'm a little behind schedule, so I don't think. . . ."

"Oh. Well, all right. Drive safely." *See also* **Blessing**.

## Straight Edge

I identified as straight edge until the end of high school, but I think the moment I stopped talking about it was after one particular show. It was at DV8 on West Temple, and featured the hardcore bands Poison the Well, Bane, and Hatebreed. The night of the show, Jacob, Karen, and I waited in line for a while, then flowed in with everyone else. We found a spot at the bottom of the stairs leading to the balcony. Bane and Poison the Well got through their sets without anything happening, but the whole time the place was vibrating, and felt like it was going to shatter. I don't know what finally started it, but during Hatebreed's set, everyone transformed into piranhas. To my right someone tried to climb the railing, only to be pulled back by fingernail force that left him bleeding; to my left someone was hit with a flying elbow and lost a tooth. Downstairs, glass broke; nobody heard it. When I think of it now, the movements look electric and fluid; a fast, poetic, almost choreographed violence. But my adrenaline moved me to flight.

Outside, broken triangles of glass sparkled on the sidewalk. I picked up a piece and put it in the pocket of my hoodie. Jacob finally exited and approached with wild eyes. "Just act normal," he said as we walked up the street. The cops were outside.

"Did you see that?" Jacob asked when we got to Dee's diner. "I beat his fucking *ass*!"

"I didn't see it," I said.

## Temple Recommend

Required to gain admittance into the temple. You get a recommend after being interviewed by the bishop and deemed worthy. (Admission of the godless into the temple would cheapen the holiness within.) Occasionally, in Utah, recommends are flashed in non-church settings to prove trustworthiness. *See also* **Marriage, Eternal.**

## Theft

a) Eventually, Brad and I were caught shoplifting. I am not sure what he took, but I was caught with Twinkies and a VHS of the movie *Magnolia.* I was taken back to school in a police car, and I had to pay a fine and take a class. I rode the bus to Provo to attend the class without telling anyone, but they wouldn't let me in without a parent or guardian present. I had to go back the next month with my horrified mother, who cried twice.

b) The story I was always told was that this was a dry, desert region undesired by all. That story might have some agricultural basis, but on a personal level, it always rubbed me the wrong way— after all, the area was already inhabited. Even if the defining feature of Utah is a dead lake, there was a fresh water lake visible from my rooftop. The people who survived on it for centuries described themselves as "fish-eaters" and "lake people." And then there were the Wasatch Mountains, which I saw the second I stepped outside my house every day. Snow-capped most of the year, and green in the spring. That area was never a desert wasteland, nor was it an area made good only because of Mormon resiliency. In many ways, just the opposite. Utah County was a long-standing paradise; as beautiful a place as any on earth. *See also* **Mormon Country**; **Zion**.

## Timpanogos

The most beloved mountain in Utah County, commonly referred to as "Timp." At the top of the 11,750-foot summit, there is a small metal structure called "the cabin." When the sun hits it, you can see a glint at the top of the mountain from all across Utah County. When the sun sets, the shadow from the mountain floods the valley, swallowing up each house one by one.

A so-called Native American legend about the mountain— actually written by a white BYU professor name Eugene Roberts— influences the way it's seen. The story tells of the sacrificial leap of a Native American princess. Influenced by this, many of us learn to visualize the outline of a dead girl on the crest of the mountain.

## Underground Panic

Toward the end of the wedding reception, I retreated into my old room in the basement. I was just standing there thinking when Chelsea came down. I don't know if she was also hiding, or if she was looking for something. We were surprised to see each other. I would like to say that I took the rare moment alone with the bride to talk about how much we loved her and how happy I was for her and Matt. But we just looked at each other, and then she said, "Well, I think I'll go back outside now."

## Unremitting Questions Everyone, Including Me, s Sick Of

Do we have to stand with Donald Trump and his ilk every time? Is it still "we"? Can we talk about what Utah County, pre-strip malls and McMansions, used to look like? Should the feeling of faith be one of certainty? Should our stories begin in the spring of 1820? If not, where? What were the sex lives of the pioneers like? Should one accept a blessing even if they don't believe? Even suppose it is all a sham. Is it worth saying it's not anyway? *See also* 1820, **Spring of;** **Blessing; Santaquin; Water.**

## Updates

On Brad: He currently works as a sous chef for a farm-to-table restaurant near Bryce Canyon National Park. The last time I visited him, he talked about taking cocaine and hallucinogens in a boat on Lake Powell—as part of a work retreat. He was always ahead of me in experiences, and I assume he always will be.

On Jacob: I do not know what happened to him, and I do not remember him fondly. He was twenty-five years old when I knew him, far too old for Karen and the other teenagers he surrounded himself with. He was eager and willing to be idolized. But he was the first non-Mormon in my life who presented a clear, ostensibly righteous path other than the one I was used to. Maybe he continued to follow it; I don't know.

On John Riel: He got married to someone I've never met, and they have at least one kid. He has a very long, Brigham Young-style beard. On Facebook, he posts Bible verses, and pictures illustrating the comical way his wife opens bags of carrots. He seems like a very nice person, and I have to say, I still resent him for that time he took me as hostage to that Christian bookstore.

On Matt and Chelsea: Still married, happily. They have two daughters: Lydia and Afton. They currently live in the house Matt and

I grew up in, while my parents are serving a second Mormon mission in Indianapolis. Matt has a podcast where he talks about movies and other nerdy topics with some of the other people we grew up with. The last time I talked to him, he told me he had been listening to some *Star Wars* short stories on the way to work, including an especially batshit one told from the perspective of a flea who entered Jabba's palace on Salacious Crumb's back, and helped Salacious ascend to the position of jester by whispering advice into his ear.

## Vision, First

The one in the sacred grove, the capital-V Vision, in which Smith heard God for the first time. We call it the First Vision, but what Smith experienced seems closer to blindness. Even in the cartoon he can't meet it head on. And what he perceives he seems to take in with a sense other than ordinary vision. Indeed, afterward, he's too stunned to take coherent action. *See also* 1820, **Spring of; Moroni.**

## Vision, Last

The initial impulse was once again to escape. According to Fawn Brodie's biography, *No Man Knows My History*, Smith, his brother Hyrum, Porter Rockwell, and Willard Richards fled Nauvoo under cover of darkness and crossed the Mississippi. The rain was thick and relentless; the downpour would have been blinding even in the day, and as they rowed across, the boat kept getting damaged by rocks they couldn't see. They had to take off their boots and bail the water out to keep from sinking.

It took all night to cross the river. When they arrived, sopping, on the other side, perhaps because there wasn't a great plan in place, perhaps because he felt he was deserting his people, Smith counseled with the others, and they rowed back and turned themselves in.

On his last day in Nauvoo, Smith rode through the town. He took in the under-construction temple and the growing young orchards. The temple was nearly complete. "This is the loveliest place and the best people under the heavens," he said. "Little do they know the trials that await them." *See also* **Orchards; "Where's Joe Smith?";** **Words, Last.**

## Water

We train ourselves to look toward the eternal mountains and away from the water. Great Salt Lake is more the salty remnant of past greatness than something great in present form. Utah Lake we've decimated through pollution. But even so, water has its way of telling stories. It teaches that some mysteries should be experienced. That some things can't be sealed. *See also* **600 Feet into Granite Mountain, A Vault; Great Salt Lake; No Water.**

## "Where's Joe Smith?"

One night during the pioneer trek, we set up camp and were enjoying a campfire competition proving who could fit the most marshmallows in his or her mouth. In the middle of the competition, some men on horseback carrying torches approached our fire. They were men from the ward, but they'd covered their faces in soot.

"Where's Joe Smith?" Brother Peters asked as they circled us with horses. "We don't take kindly to you people here. You Mormons better get out of here tonight, or you'll all die."

We had to pick up camp and go to another location. During testimony meeting the next day, Brother Huntzinger, one of the organizers of the trek, talked about how furious he was at first that they had done that without informing him. "But then I realized," he said, tears forming in his eyes, "that's what the pioneers went through all the time." *See also* **Facing Zion; Pioneer Day.**

## Words, Last

The militia, their faces painted black, waited until the governor was out of town, and then ambushed Carthage jail. They rushed past the guards and ran upstairs where the cell was. Hyrum and Richards tried to lean against the wooden door and keep them out, but the muskets and bayonets burst through the wood and filled the cell with gunfire. Hyrum was shot and killed. John Taylor, who would later become prophet, was shot but not killed because the bullet hit his pocket watch.

Smith stepped up to the window, and, looking for an escape, saw only torches and bayonets below.

According to William Daniels, one of the militia men, he was hit while looking out the window and fell. His last words were "Oh Lord, my God!" The fall didn't kill him, but four men lifted him up and fired at him to finish him off.

When we toured the jail as a family, this scene was recreated via an audio recording on a portable CD player. Loud gun shots, and voice actors playing the parts of the prophet and the others. The tour guide stayed silent after it finished playing and left us with our thoughts.

## X

Things I never admitted to my mother during those teenage years, when I was drawing X's on my hands and smelled of black hair dye and sweat: I was lonely. Occasionally my worldly choices tasted as bitter as she suggested they would. I felt like a fraud because I knew I couldn't even approximate the intensity of the other straight edgers. I still prayed sometimes. Heart of hearts, I didn't really care about sobriety. *See also* **Beliefs; Straight Edge.**

## Young, Brigham

Some thought the church would disband after Smith died, but being murdered by a mob transformed Smith into a martyr and a legend. Brigham Young, with the priesthood passed to him, became the second prophet of the church, and eventually the first governor of Utah.

Young was famous for his literal-mindedness, his beard, and for having even more wives (fifty-five) than Smith. He was also the one to enforce the ban on black men being ordained with the priesthood, which lasted until 1978.

A small park has been constructed around his gravesite in Salt Lake City, the location of which bordered my old apartment building. In the park, there is a statue of a bronze Brigham Young sitting on a bench reading the scriptures to some bronze children peering over his shoulder. A few years ago, vandals managed to loosen and steal the welded book, so for a while, he was holding nothing. Or, you could put whatever book you wanted there—*Soul on Ice, Ariel, Lolita*—

though none of them fit perfectly in his hand. The best fit was a collected anthology of Golden Age *Wonder Woman* comics. A series of photos show me leaning in with the bronze children as Brother Young reads to us from different books.

## Young Joseph Smith

The early years are by far Smith's most endearing. The desire for treasure, for a way out of the hard-ass labor of tending a rocky farm, for excitement and pleasure and fame. The hope for miracles and the confidence to make them happen. The world he created would eventually grow wide enough to hold thousands of loyal followers. But the adult Smith is someone I can't really abide. Young Joseph Smith was someone I might have been able to follow, at least for a while. *See also* **Excitement.**

## Zion

After being driven out of everywhere else, the Mormon Zion ended up being in Utah. With due respect to the previous stops, this was a much better Zion than the sweaty Midwest. Because of the mountains, it's difficult to ruin, despite strong efforts. Any time you feel despair, you just have to look up. *See also* **Timpanogos; Water.**

## Zion from My Rearview Mirror

The day after the wedding, I got back in my car to drive away. I was relieved to escape, even as I grieved anew the reality of fleeing the place I once thought I'd never leave. I watched the mountains in my rearview mirror as I drove west toward the freeway. The sun blazed on Timpanogos and I knew exactly where I was. I don't think I'll ever feel that certainty in another place. I turned left and then merged onto I-15 South. *See also* **Dreams; Distance to Texas; Exile; Facing Zion; Faith; Heavens; Infant in the Water; Orientation; No Job; Post-Mormon; Santaquin; Sluff; Timpanogos; Unremitting Questions Everyone, Including Me, Is Sick Of; Water; Zion.**

# Point Guard

I.

A few notes on John Stockton, my childhood idol:

- He grew up in Spokane, the son of a bar owner. Sportswriters often describe him as looking like a "choir boy." He was literally an altar boy. He was raised in part by the Sisters of the Holy Name.

- He had a reputation as one of the dirtiest players in the NBA. At a game's beginning, he would run his knee into the player screening him to discourage hard screens in the future. When setting backscreens of his own, he would make his elbows knives. He crushed enough backs that the league eventually made it a point of emphasis for referees to watch for his style of screening. He stood obnoxiously close to players he defended, even during stoppages, to make them uncomfortable.

- He had impeccable conditioning throughout his career. At six foot one and 175 pounds, he played until he was forty-one years old. In nineteen years, he missed only twenty-two games. He had huge hands and great vision. He is the NBA's all-time leader in assists (15,806) and steals (3,265).

- He hated signing autographs. The stories of him shouting at people approaching with a pen and paper, including children, are legion. He was drafted #16 overall in the 1984 draft, which also included Michael Jordan, Hakeem Olajuwon, and Charles Barkley. He wore short shorts as a rookie and still wore them when he retired nineteen years later.

- Perhaps each of these should be its own bullet point. A clean list of stats and facts. But that is not how I think about Stockton. As a child I loved him with such intensity that I wept when he lost, and afterward walked around bowed with sadness, not only for myself, but for him. A chart of his career from my perspective is messier than a cumulative list. It also has to account for loss.

❖ He is probably best known for never winning a championship. He, along with Charles Barkley and teammate Karl Malone, are the first names that come up in a discussion of great players who never won it all.

2.

It's difficult to get into Stockton's head. His answers when interviewed are mostly standard athlete-speak, and his autobiography likewise relies on platitudes.

❖ For example: "Success is too often seen in terms of wealth and fame. My parents had neither, but they are my heroes." In that book, he claims to have left a party as a teenager when he found out kids were drinking. When he talks about games, he tends to recount only what happened at the end. For as many stats as he accumulated, he never mentions numbers. He talks about learning tendencies through repetition and film, but never gives specifics. He writes that "every lesson I ever learned on the court seemed to find its way into my life," but again gives no examples.

❖ I sometimes wonder if Stockton feels what he's saying, or if he's just trying to deliver the most efficacious message. For example, at one point in his autobiography, he claims that Karl Malone was just reacting to a fake when he fouled Isiah Thomas so hard he cut open his face. Stockton describes it as a hard foul, unrelated to the controversy about Stockton making the Olympic team over Thomas. He sounds like he's still trying to limit Malone's potential fine or suspension through public comments. Decades later, with those penalties long since handed out, it's hard to believe that's really how he perceives it.

❖ During his career, he would sometimes sound less polished and more melancholy in the locker room immediately after a loss. After a playoff loss to the eventual-champion Lakers in 1988, in which he'd scored fourteen points and handed out seventeen assists, he was asked if he could take any satisfaction from his individual performance. "You can find satisfaction in anything if you want to. The world is full of satisfied losers. The thing that matters is where you choose to draw the line at what you're satisfied with."

## 3.

Stockton was my favorite player then, and Russell Westbrook is my favorite player now (not counting Jazz players).

❖ It's tempting to present this as evidence of how my outlook has changed—what I had been taught to value contrasted with what I learned to value. The glory of silent hard work vs. the exuberance of play (while still working hard).

❖ Stockton made all of his teammates better, and played the game "the right way." He never boasted, just did his job. He would always trade a decent look of his own for a better shot from a teammate.

❖ In contrast, Westbrook struggles to find open teammates, even teammates as good as Kevin Durant or James Harden. But he can grab a defensive rebound, blur down the floor, and hammer a dunk over anyone who doesn't move out of his way. He will say something about it after doing so.

❖ The two players have very different styles. But in some ways, the experience of pulling for Westbrook reminds me of pulling for Stockton. A long career with a single team and a crazed fanbase, marked thus far by coming up short.

## 4.

In 1998, the Jazz made the Finals for the second straight year. Unlike in 1997, they had homecourt advantage. They were also rested and healthy; they were coming off a sweep of the Lakers, while the Bulls had just ground out a seven-game series with the Pacers. I was pulling for Indiana in that series; I was terrified of Jordan and Pippen.

* We loved that team. Jazz flags hung in windows and cars throughout the state. Our family changed the spelling of our cat's name from Jasmine to Jazzmine. When the Finals started, I made a vow with God that I would never fake being sick to get out of church again if the Jazz won.

* They lost in six. Like most Jazz fans, I was haunted by Game Six for years afterward. Pippen, who had single-handedly wrecked our offense for two straight years, was hurt. He missed some of Game Six, and wasn't moving like he usually did. In the second quarter, Howard Eisley made a three-pointer that was waved off for being a shot clock violation, but it wasn't. (This was before instant replay.) In the fourth quarter, Ron Harper released a shot after the shot clock had expired that counted but shouldn't have. And then of course there is Jordan's last shot. Jordan's form, as always, was beautiful, with a posed follow-through, suggesting he knew that was going to be his last iconic moment. But to get that open, he threw Bryon Russell to the ground.

5.

Mormons love basketball. Most Utahns do. That love is one of few things in the state that can unite the faithful and unfaithful.

* Nearly every Mormon church has a basketball gym inside. By 10th Grade, my skills were too poor to compete in high school, so for me it was only church ball from that point forward. Even after I stopped attending church, I still showed up for basketball.

* Church ball is supposed to be a wholesome, bonding activity, but it's notoriously competitive and poorly refereed. Swearing is, for once, overlooked.

* I don't remember when I learned Stockton wasn't Mormon, but I remember being surprised. He talks just like one and espouses similar values. In his book, he notes that while

his dad described him as being "tighter than the bark on a tree," his frugality and saving habits "literally paid dividends down the line." He jokes the same way my dad does and is similarly free-wheeling with exclamation points. He spent part of his honeymoon at Disneyland, for hell's sake.

- ❖ And he plays like a Mormon too. Or we play like him. He seized basketball as an outlet where he could compete, just as church ball players do, as hard as possible and by any means necessary. Is it dirty to blindside a player with a hard backscreen he doesn't anticipate? What it *is* is effective.

- ❖ One of my priesthood teachers had a story about church ball that ended with a roundhouse kick. In the story, a would-be convert is being hounded on defense throughout the game. His defender is talking trash and hacking at him. Eventually, the would-be convert has had enough. He kicks his harasser, thanks the person who invited him, but says this isn't for him. Our teacher thought the takeaway was that we should play respectfully and keep the big picture in mind, but he missed the point of his own story. The defender got that player to leave the game. A pure Stockton move.

- ❖ We were never able to convert Stockton to the Church, despite nineteen years in Utah. But I'm sure his name has already been put in for thousands of baptisms after he dies.

### 6.

Some notes on choosing favorite players:

- ❖ It seems that sometimes people mistake "favorite" for "best." For example, when I say Westbrook is my favorite player, some fans will outline the ways that Westbrook could be better: if he would trust his teammates a little more, hunt stats less, or place less reliance on long pull-up jumpers.

- ❖ I don't disagree. But that isn't the point.

- ❖ According to Stockton, "Competitive athletics should be a metaphor for real life." He probably meant that teamwork applied both on the court and in the boardroom, or something like that, but taken seriously, that is the quote I consider when choosing a favorite player. It's about identifying a way of being and a style you admire through play. For Stockton and Westbrook, it's not all virtuous, but it's valuable to me.

7.

Say we do attend to Stockton and Westbrook not just as people, but as metaphors. What do they represent?

* For Stockton: toughness. The willingness to play through anything. Extreme preparation and conditioning. Action over words.

* For Westbrook: effort, heart, and individuality triumphing over professionalism and conformity.

* For both of them: consistency. Stockton's first professional coach, Frank Layden, told him: "Don't change who you are now that you've arrived," and he didn't. Likewise, Westbrook plays on fire regardless of context, commentary, or past result. For better and worse. I'm sure Westbrook could have found Durant for a few more open 3s. And I wouldn't have minded Stockton taking a few more himself, instead of dishing them out to David Benoit, no matter how open.

* For both of them: sexiness. Westbrook, anyway, is unabashedly fashionable and handsome. Is short-shorts Stockton also sexy? I say yes.

* They might also be metaphors for failing spectacularly.

8.

In his autobiography, Stockton notes that when he tries to recall specific games from the Finals, "my recollection often blurs—perhaps as a protective mechanism against reliving the pain of losing."

Even though I remembered it clearly enough for haunting, I didn't watch Game 6 again until many years later. I averted my eyes at even the highlight of Jordan's last shot.

By the time I re-watched it, I did so in one of the green seats that

103

had been in the arena at the time. I purchased a pair of them when the Jazz renovated the arena.

A few notes from the game:

- ❖ The broadcasters are Bob Costas, Doug Collins (Jordan's former coach), and Isiah Thomas (Stockton's most admired colleague, the one whose head Malone split open). Thomas seems nervous somehow, stumbling over his words in an opening segment.

- ❖ The NBA on NBC theme song, much beloved by me as a child, still bangs.

- ❖ Seeing Jordan and Pippen warm up, the fear rushes back.

- ❖ Everybody who has watched the NBA for a long time is vaguely aware of this, but it's striking how much the game has transformed since the nineties. Even despite the illegal defense rules of the time, there are multiple Bulls near the paint on every possession. Both teams play so many non-shooters at once.

- ❖ I had forgotten that Sloan started Adam Keefe. I'd expected to see Ostertag, who struggled in that series, out there. Or at least Foster. Keefe does not play well.

- ❖ The Jazz are a conspicuously white team. I cannot remember what I did with that information as a kid. I'm sure I was aware of it.

- ❖ Pippen throws down a dunk early, but leaves the game shortly thereafter to get treatment on his back. He's grimacing.

- ❖ The Bulls had a big edge at the free-throw line in the series, but not in this game. And the illegal defense they played, much complained about by Sloan, is called a few times.

- ❖ The post-up positioning is violent on both sides. A lot of strength and elbows. Everyone tries to post-up Hornacek.

- ❖ Jeff Foster grabs a defensive rebound, but bungles the exchange with Eisley and the ball goes out of bounds. On the next possession, Foster throws it away. "That's two atrocious turnovers by Foster on consecutive possessions," Costas says.

❖ Costas, taking a break from the action: "NBC gives you double Frasiers every week."

❖ There's Eisley's waived-off 3. It really was a prayer—a thirty-footer on the run. And it wasn't even all that close to being a shot clock violation.

❖ The Jazz offense, still cluttered at times, runs much more smoothly with Pippen out.

❖ Of course, I remember Stockton checking out halfway through the first quarter and returning in the second, as he did for years. But it is notable just how much of the game he misses. He plays just thirty-three minutes. Malone plays forty-three; Jordan forty-four.

❖ With Pippen out, the announcers are wondering how much Jordan can carry. "If he doesn't step up, other than Kukoč, who else can?"

❖ I'm convinced God's favorite shot would look exactly like Jordan's fadeaway baseline jumper.

❖ The refs do not call many fouls in what Costas calls "a choppy third quarter."

❖ Jordan, who normally rested at the beginning of the fourth quarter, stays out there with his team trailing by five.

❖ Malone and Rodman get tangled under the basket, and keep running into each other and falling down as they run back up the court. Rodman is called for a foul. Costas pleads for a flagrant foul on Rodman, but watching the replay, there's nothing there.

❖ Malone has a great game. He scores thirty-one points on 11-19 shooting, 9-11 from the line. He has eleven rebounds and seven assists, and plays great defense. His reputation among some as an overrated player who choked in big moments is not based on this game.

- Rodman hits a twenty-footer, a shot I never would have guessed him trying, and does the Jordan shrug.

- Malone loses the ball in the lane, wanting a foul. A mic picks up a fan yelling "Call that illegal defense!" on the broadcast.

- Steve Kerr opens Kukoč for a 3 by setting a screen, and Malone does not even try to run around it. He just barrels through Kerr. No call is made, but Kukoč buries the 3.

- When Stockton shoots, he cocks the ball to the right of his head. I used to try to imitate the motion, but could never make it work.

- There's Harper's shot, the one that shouldn't have counted. Unlike the Eisley one, this one is very close.

- Just as I had as a child, and even recalling that doing so had burned us in the past, I find myself pleading for someone to double-team Michael Jordan.

- Stockton misses an open jumper and an open 3 on consecutive possessions. Then Malone finds him for another 3, and he buries it. He finishes 4-10 from the field.

- As he had done the previous year, Jordan steals the ball from Malone in a key moment. The Jazz have a one-point lead and throw it to Malone in the post. When Hornacek makes his cut behind Malone, the defending Jordan does not follow him all the way through. He lingers under the basket, then sneaks in and swipes the ball cleanly.

- Jordan's push-off, in real time, is less criminal than I'd remembered. Russell goes flying, but without slow motion, you can't even see Jordan's arm extend, he's so subtle. It's a Stockton-esque trick that I have to admire.

- "If that's the last image of MJ, how magnificent is it?" Costas says.

- But there are five seconds left. We still have a chance to win. On the final play, Stockton's shot, well-defended by Ron

Harper, looks like it's going in. It falls short.

- ❖ In the postgame interviews—which are marked by Jim Gray and Ahmad Rashad almost pleading with the Chicago ownership, management, coaches, and players to commit to coming back next year—everyone on Chicago is gracious about Utah. Reinsdorf says, "It's unfortunate it can't be co-champions." Jordan shouts out the Utah fans, saying that they dreaded coming back to Utah because of their energy. Pippen makes similar comments.

- ❖ Both of them are worn out.

- ❖ "Of all the championships that we've won, this is the toughest," Jordan says.

## 9.

Jordan is the dream killer, but I've had nightmares about Scottie Pippen as well. No player is capable of eclipsing Jordan in my imagination, but if I were to make the argument for LeBron, I would start by talking about Scottie Pippen.

- ❖ He messed up our whole thing. He would either float on defense and disrupt everything, or Jackson would put him on Stockton, who would struggle to initiate the offense around his length. He always knew exactly what we were trying to do.

- ❖ The year after Jordan retired the first time, the Bulls won fifty-five games—just two fewer than the previous year. They added Toni Kukoč as a rookie, but otherwise they simply lost the greatest player ever and didn't replace him. They lost in the second round to the Knicks. In Game Three, Pippen took himself out of the game after Jackson called the last play for Kukoč. The play worked, and Pippen probably shouldn't have done that. But I can understand his frustration, as that play call was emblematic of his career: he was always paid and treated like a sidekick, when he was one of the game's greatest players in his own right.

❖ "When Michael is out there on the court, I look to be more aggressive defensively because I feel that I can create things on the defensive end that he can do on the offensive end," Pippen said after Game Three in 1998, the only game in either of the Jazz-Bulls Finals that wasn't close. The Bulls won 96–54.

### 10.

Much of what Stockton stands for can also be said of Karl Malone, whom I haven't mentioned much at all: They both have statues in front of the arena, and streets named after them. Jazz fans, loyal to Malone, still call him the greatest power forward to ever play the game—even if they have to make caveats about Tim Duncan being more of a true center, anyway.

❖ In 2008, Jemele Hill wrote a story about Malone's unclaimed son, Demetress Bell. Malone reportedly impregnated Bell's mother when she was thirteen years old and he was a sophomore in college. He denied paternity and ditched child support, even after he made the NBA.

❖ I don't know what I would have done with this information had I known it in the nineties. It's hard to untangle and disavow all that passion. I likely would have rationalized it. Malone did a lot for the community. He was a philanthropist and a notoriously generous tipper. His own father committed suicide when he was three. It was a long time ago.

❖ But I can't get there. I don't expect or want athletes to be role models. But I was upset to see fans deify Kobe Bryant after he was accused of rape. Perhaps my position should be more nuanced; perhaps morality should not factor in at all. But if cheering for a player is a matter of choosing representations of what is good and valuable in life, I can't cheer for Malone.

### 11.

Sometimes I wonder what would have happened if Stockton had made that shot—if we got a Game Seven at home with Pippen injured.

❖ Maybe we would have won. Maybe my life would have changed. Maybe I would have applied to elite colleges in high school, assuming anything was possible. Maybe I'd still be an active Mormon.

❖ It's also possible that we were the villains in another story all along. The Bulls played with tremendous heart. Pippen, underrated and underpaid throughout his career, found a way to be out there and create a key steal in the fourth quarter. Jordan saved his energy so he could make just enough plays at the end.

❖ In the movie *Hoosiers*, we root for Hickory High in part because theirs is the story we know. But it feels a little as though we're supposed to be more impressed by them than the team from South Bend they defeat because, unlike that team of black players, the white Hoosiers weren't born with all the talent in the world. They had to work to get where they were.

❖ Why was our team so white? Was it just a coincidence? Did management consciously or otherwise prefer white players? Did they say something about wanting players who represented certain "values" and actually mean white? Was it the market? Did we, the fans, respond more passionately to a team with a lot of white players?

❖ Just last year, Westbrook got into a confrontation with a fan in Utah who was shouting racist taunts from the stands. "I swear to God, I'll fuck you up. You and your wife, I'll fuck you up," Westbrook responded. The fan was thrown out and received a lifetime ban.

❖ After the event, the consensus was that nobody behaved well, but as usual, Westbrook's response was just fine by me.

❖ What's startling about the video isn't just what the fan shouts at Westbrook; it's the fact that nobody around him says anything about it. Maybe that's more who we are than I like to admit. If so, our losing really wasn't so tragic.

## 12.

I still love the Jazz. I can't help it. Basketball is the last burning ember from my childhood religion. The team is no longer conspicuously white, and I hope we're past that. I hope we will continue to throw racist fans out of the stadium. I'd still keep that vow to God if He put a championship on the table. In the meantime, I'll continue trying to figure out where to draw the line for how much loss I can accept—and what to do when that line is crossed.

# 7-Eleven Clerk, Again

During my last two semesters of college, I took out a student loan, quit my job at 7-Eleven, and focused entirely on school. The difference between going to school without a job and going to school while working was like comparing a game of HORSE to full-court basketball. It was hard for me to accept that the work was graded the same way in both scenarios. I was never worn out, and had time for everything. I volunteered to work on a literary journal and took philosophy classes for fun. After classes, I hung around the green couches in the Liberal Arts Building and read beyond what was required. Sometimes I'd stay late enough to fist-bump my former vacuum specialist colleagues when they showed up, including my replacement. It was a year of college leisure.

In the winter of that year, I applied to some MFA programs for creative writing—another thing I likely wouldn't have had time to do if I'd been working. But I didn't get in anywhere initially—at least not with funding. I was accepted to the University of Utah, but only if I could pay my own way. I had been wait-listed at the University of Wyoming, and firmly rejected everywhere else. Despite the lack of funding, I indicated to Utah that I planned to attend. Even as I did so, I felt that I might ultimately have to bail. I held off on actually making that decision as long as possible—and I probably would have held off right until I calculated the first tuition bill. But someone above me on the list at Utah must have chosen another school, which meant I got bumped up into a funded position.

In retrospect, I was very lucky. I remember editing the piece I submitted as my writing sample at the library the day the postmark was due. It was a fifteen-page piece about my friends who had drowned—with my entire life story thrown in for good measure. Utah's program taught me how to improve it, but at the time of my application, I got in on potential and luck and a strong recommendation from one professor.

~

In the meantime, I graduated and it was summer. I needed to move to Salt Lake City, but couldn't convince Anna to go with me. Suddenly, she loved Utah County. It seemed we'd always talked about leaving for a glossier destination, but now she wasn't feeling it. True, she still had a year of classes to take at UVSC. She also said she liked her small apartment and being able to walk everywhere she needed to go. I spent weeks trying to talk her into moving, but we were mirroring the same arguments back and forth to each other. I didn't want to commute the forty-five miles, either. I felt that if I lived in Utah County, I wouldn't ever be part of the program. She felt that if she moved, she would lose the community she had, with no identity in Salt Lake beyond being someone's partner.

I couldn't move her, and didn't want to risk not having a place to live at the start of fall semester, so I made plans to move in with a friend from college named Breanne. She had been a Mormon missionary in New York City on 9/11 and that was a big part of her identity, as was the fact that she'd been the first woman student-body president at Bingham High School. We moved into a green brick apartment complex called the Plaza, an embodiment of the 1970s, with a dumpster on the front lawn. Our two-bedroom apartment was on the third floor and had a balcony. Split two ways, the rent wasn't bad. The apartments were in decent shape, though the landlords were very hard to track down when repairs were needed. At one point toward the end, I recall a crack in the window being taped over with an OBAMA sticker.

~

After the move, and my year as a full-time student, I had no money left, not even enough to get me through the summer, after which I would have a teaching position at Utah. I needed a job. Walking around one day, I saw a Now Hiring sign in the 7-Eleven bordering campus. On the spot, I stepped in and applied. The store was transitioning from being a corporate-run store to a franchise, run by the Khatri family. Some of the old employees were transferring elsewhere as a result, and they needed someone to work the graveyard shift. I'd done it before, and that was enough. I don't think they called my references.

My new 7-Eleven was basically the same as the old one. Same strategy for keeping the safe stocked and the cash in the register low. Even the freezer in the back looked mostly the same, with the gleaming sodas pointing west instead of north. Again, cops came through all night because we gave them free drinks. Some light differences: a new model of soda machine with flashy, slot-machine lights that allowed customers to inject extra vanilla or lemon flavor into their sodas. A portable CD player behind the cash register. There were steps behind the store that led up to the University of Utah, instead of just a dumpster. There was a halfway house around the corner, and proximity to the university meant there were more students. But even then, it was the summer. It was dead.

～

The biggest change was the boss. Because this 7-Eleven was franchised by a family, the only fellow employees I met were Khatris. They all worked there in some capacity: husband, wife, son (around sixteen), daughter (around twelve). The patriarch was more hands-on than my old boss, and showed a temper. During my first week, he said the following:

1. "Even thugs like *him* (nodding to tattooed customer) won't rob us if we say hello when they walk in."

2. [Slamming his fists on a cardboard box of soda for the machine]: "More fucking Hawaiian Punch!"

3. "You will be married one day and understand my anger."

Working with family members was much worse than working with the gas station attendants I was used to, who mostly shared a motto of wanting to be left alone to brood in peace. Family members didn't have that option. How were children going to openly scoff at their family's livelihood? As a result, they were passionate when someone stole a case of beer and ran up the stairs into an escape vehicle—instead of just shrugging it off. Their lack of apathy was understandable, but I still wished those kids would slack a little more.

But I worked most of my shift alone. I would show up at 11:00 p.m. and stay until 7:00 a.m. When I arrived at 11:00, whichever family members were there would stay for as long as they needed to tie up loose ends—sometimes no more than a minute, sometimes an hour. It was always a relief after they left, and I didn't have to look busy or keep an eye out for shoplifters. I would put in my eight hours and then see the Khatris again in the morning.

∿

I was grateful to be in the MFA program. I felt validated, and it gave me a clear direction I hadn't had since I was a believing Mormon. But I was terrified. Of everything—being exposed as a hack in workshop, having to make friends, major gaps in my reading. More than anything, I was afraid of teaching classes. I had never once shown a talent for teaching; in group work in college, I was always the dead weight, and I had a tendency to shake with panic any time I had to speak in public. I was twenty-three and I knew "my" students would see me for the fraud I was. At Sev, the customers called me "sport," "bud," or sometimes "boss." Nobody was going to call me "professor"—or whatever I was supposed to ask them to call me, considering I didn't have any advanced degrees.

When nothing was happening at work, I wrote down what I was thinking about. Sometimes these notes were ideas for stories, plans to coax Anna north, or lists of books to read. But I almost always ended up writing about my fear of teaching. I sometimes wondered if I'd be better off back in Utah County, just getting high with Anna and hanging out, which is what I would have done if Utah hadn't admitted me. Maybe I'd be back at the call center, or even another 7-Eleven—some job that I knew how to do.

With Anna and all my friends and family in Utah County, my life mattered to a small and fading set of people. I knew Breanne, but she had her own life. Other than her, my only friend in Salt Lake was Steve. He was also from Utah County, and I had known him for over ten years. His strongest traits were contempt for bullying, and a ruthless intolerance for self-delusion, to the point that I would revise my stories mid-telling if I felt like I was depicting myself as too much of a hero or victim. In high school, he sometimes wore blue Dickies coveralls to school. He had a temper, but not the childish sort. I once saw our friend Chaz hit him in the shoulder in frustration, and Steve just stared him down. I think he was the only practicing Mormon left standing by the time our group of friends graduated high school. He was good-natured about this, playfully making fun of our reasons for not going to church: "My bishop was mean; now I don't believe in God." In college, he moved into honor code apartments in Provo, a code he broke whenever he played video games and unleashed profanity so intense that it surprised even me. He broke it again whenever his girlfriend Tamara slept over. He had just finished his associate's degree at UVSC and transferred to Utah to finish his bachelor's.

Coincidentally, and to my great luck, he lived one street over from 7-Eleven. After my shift was over, I would walk up to his apartment. If I saw a light on, I would knock and invite myself in for coffee. We would talk for a while, often while he was getting ready. Then he would go to work, and I would take the bus home.

~

A man who lived at the halfway house around the block asked if he could fill up a bucket with ice. Perhaps I was supposed to charge him, or just say no, but I didn't. I had been pretty cavalier about protocol my first time around at Sev, but knowing that I would be gone in months left me truly free to not give a shit.

I came to regret the choice because the man came in often after that first encounter. In July it was in the nineties every day. A perpetual need for ice outside, though the store itself was always a little too cold. He would fill up his bucket, and then hang around and talk. He asked what I was playing on the CD player and then added that he himself was a musician—a bassist.

"Should have played lead guitar, though," he said. "More pussy that way." Semi-vulgar sentences of that nature were a part of working a graveyard shift, but I remember that one in particular because he winked when he said it. He added, "I bet you know what I'm talking about."

"I don't play any instruments," I lied. I didn't want to bring the trombone into it.

~

In a way, the graveyard shift was perfect for the time because I couldn't sleep anyway. It wasn't just my body's inevitable readjustment to a night shift. I was anxious enough that I couldn't fall asleep unless I was completely drained or drunk. I had a constant fear that one of the young people in 7-Eleven would be in my class later, and remember me. And a more general fear that I would get laughed out of the classroom. Fired for incompetence and thrown out of the program. I didn't learn until later just how bad a teacher one could be without repercussion—nobody was in any hurry to find a substitute for a graduate student willing to teach a class cheap. But I didn't know that yet. I assumed all teachers were well-prepared and sharp. That thought, contrasted with my own life, panicked me. Mixed with the adjustment of the graveyard sleep schedule, I had a terrible time falling asleep.

~

Once, the exhaustion caught up to me and I slept through my alarm and missed the beginning of my shift. When I woke up and saw the missed calls, I lied and said I'd been in a car accident (thankfully not too serious). The entire family had waited an extra hour and a half for me to show up. They believed my story or pretended to. They asked if I could work later in the morning so they could sleep a bit more, and I said yes.

~

That lie was the most eventful thing that happened all summer. Without students, the 7-Eleven was mostly loitering cops, halfway house residents, and the occasional group of drunk white boys—young people feeling their oats so much that they mistook 7-Eleven for Las Vegas. But even they couldn't sustain the illusion for long and never lingered. For the most part I was left to dread visions of standing in front of a class of skeptics, filling 50 minutes with talk.

~

Rather than throw them away, I put the day-old doughnuts on the counter and gave them away for free before the morning delivery of the new batch. Most people politely declined when I offered them. Then, around 3:30 a.m., one man came in and took them all. He put the cake donuts on his index and middle fingers like rings and carried the rest out. He didn't buy anything else, just took the doughnuts and left, as if he knew they were waiting for him. Then the store was empty again.

~

"So you see what you're missing by not stopping by," I said to Steve in the morning. I had invited him to come by the store during one of my shifts, and told him I'd let him shoplift whatever he wanted, as long as he could be subtle for the camera. He said he would stop by some night he didn't have to work the next morning.

~

Two weeks before the semester started, I had to take a mandatory, week-long orientation about teaching composition. It went from nine to five, Monday to Friday, for one week. My shift at 7-Eleven ended at 7:00 a.m., so I had to load up on coffee and steel myself for orientation right afterward. The exhaustion was probably not an ideal way to start, but on the plus side, I was too tired to be as worried about it as I normally would have been. After the orientation, I would go home, sleep for four hours, and do it again.

There were probably twenty-five people in that orientation—each one teaching composition for the first time at Utah, though nearly all the others had taught elsewhere before. I remember only one person with no experience, but she was a confident former actor with clear and repeatedly mentioned plans to incorporate acting techniques in the classroom. In addition, everyone seemed to be a real adult. They carried satchels instead of backpacks and wore stylish shoes. I wore T-shirts and the same red high-tops as always. I had planned to buy something more professional by the time classes started, but hadn't found the time by orientation.

If the room had been full of people like me, nobody would have said anything and the prepared sections would have seemed woefully thin for filling eight hours. But they were designed assuming we would bring and share our own experience and expertise. And everyone, except me, had stories. One person complained she had taught "A Modest Proposal" and her students hadn't recognized it as satire. Others gave helpful examples of how they illustrated argumentative fallacies using examples from popular culture. I made a note to look up what those fallacies were. I vaguely knew I had been taught that in my own composition class, but I could not remember. I took notes on everything. I kept my mouth shut unless forced to participate. I was trying to adopt a persona of someone who watched things closely, as a writer might, even if I didn't do anything with what I observed.

∿

One night, early into orientation week, Steve did stop in during my shift. He didn't steal anything, though I insisted on giving him a soda from the machine. He stayed for about an hour, talking about his own job delivering paint. He had recently brought a delivery to the KSL building downtown and seen some of the news anchors in person. It was wonderful to have him. The details of his own work-related tedium comforted me, and none of the customers lingered while he was there.

∿

The leader of the orientation, and director of the Rhetoric and Composition department, was a woman named Jolene. I picked up quickly that the others found her to be misguided and condescending. We each had assigned "books" we had to use—packets of essays Jolene judged to be effective for teaching rhetoric. One of them was themed on the environment, the other on the economy. We were given our choice of the two. There was much complaining about these packets—though for my part, I still approached the texts as I would have as a student. They could have contained anything and I would have believed they were worthwhile, if handed to me by an English teacher.

The others, through experience, were more cynical—enough so that they would gently mock the content of the orientation during lunch, and complain about the fact that we weren't being paid to be there. I was so stressed about the event itself I forgot to question that.

We were all required to teach the same four assignments: an annotated bibliography, a report, a rhetorical analysis, and an argument. Beyond that, we were free to structure the classes as we wanted—as long as we also used the reading packets. One student wanted to use Martin Luther King Jr.'s "Letter from Birmingham Jail" to teach rhetorical analysis. Jolene said she didn't think the letter was necessarily an academic text, which led to much pushback and some frustrated snark. As the week went on, smiles began to fade when Jolene would speak. I didn't mind her that much myself, but I was grateful to have a common enemy.

∼

During orientation week, I spent good portions of my shift at Sev walking back to the freezer, just to snap myself awake. The late night felt like the early morning and at all times I felt like a slight breeze could hurl me into an emotional breakdown. I would check out customers in silence because I didn't want them to detect anything in my voice.

Midway through that week, I walked into the room and saw the desks had been formed into small circles. I nearly wept. We worked in small groups role-playing teaching different material to students. In one of the role play activities, I remember saying something like, "Plagiarism . . . well, that's not so good."

For lunch, the entire group went to the Pie for pizza. My slice didn't come out with the others, and I had to inquire about it. They then handed me a slice with a single, uncooked tomato slice on top. I was the last one eating.

The day finally wound down, and I heard the glorious sound of Jolene's tone changing to indicate the close of the day (unless anyone had anything they wanted to add)—at which point someone blew my mind by actually speaking. What was said, I'm not sure, since asking a question after that tone change was as baffling to me as if she had spoken in tongues. I wouldn't have asked for my kidney back if it meant extending orientation, but whatever the comment was, it led to a robust, fifteen-minute discussion.

∼

With just two orientation days left, I was exhausted and felt only slightly more equipped to teach composition than when the week had started. I left my shift at Sev and walked toward Steve's apartment. His light wasn't on, but I knocked anyway. When he answered, it was clear I'd woken him. Nevertheless, he invited me in. He made some coffee while I showed him my student/faculty ID. Before the picture was taken, I had tried to comb my hair for the first time all summer, even using a black picture-day comb, and indeed I looked like an eight-year-old child.

"I don't think I can do this, man. I'm not like the other teachers. It isn't natural for me."

"Just relax. You can do it."

"You've known me a long time, and I doubt you've ever heard me say more than five words to a group. There's no way."

"I'm sure it would help if you could be a little less aware about it. But look, it's still just a job. Take it one day at a time. Clock in, clock out. Just show up, and you'll be fine."

〜

I was so bad at teaching that first semester that I immediately tried to block the students from my mind, so that if they ever recognized me in public, I would have plausible deniability. This despite wanting to buy each of them a bouquet of flowers. If not for the goodness of those students, my class would have completely fallen apart. I was like a bad stand-up act that they, through sheer force of will, thought they could help. But overall, Steve's terms helped me. Each class, I tried to put together enough of a lesson plan to get me through fifty minutes. Then I would hold office hours and grade. I treated it like a shift at Sev—hours clocked and a to-do list. It wasn't *Stand and Deliver*. But I wasn't fired. I killed time with chit-chat before starting into the lecture plan. I had my students do a lot of in-class writing. We watched *Buffy* episodes and I had them write letters to friends they hadn't talked to in over a year. I had them write arguments persuading someone to move to Salt Lake from another part of the state. I assigned them readings from the packet, but often didn't lecture on them in class. The semester ended. Nobody's tuition was refunded, as that is not an option. By the end of the semester, I met Steve for breakfast and told him that his approach had worked—I'd survived the class and felt I could do it again. He put his arm on my shoulder and said, "Good for you, Professor Motherfucker."

~

Just about a year later, right before he was about to graduate, Steve shot himself in the head. I know it is jarring and possibly unethical to drop this information so late in a piece that's been about petty anxiety to this point. But whenever I think of Steve now, I almost can't help starting in the desert where his life ended, before working my way back. I wanted to try to write about him the way it was before that, when nothing was going on, and he was eating toast, complaining about his co-workers, putting on his paint-splattered shoes.

~

Ever since I was hired at 7-Eleven, I'd planned to quit as soon as the semester started. Of course, I didn't mention that. When I put in my two weeks' notice, Mr. Khatri seemed personally offended. "Is there something wrong? You don't like it here?"

"It's not that. I just got into school at the last minute." Once again, I lied to his face and hoped it would hold, and either it did, or he just let it go. "Well, we wish you the best," he said.

My last night at 7-Eleven, a man walked in and made his way toward the refrigerated sandwiches. He had his back to me, and I wasn't looking at him directly anyway. From my periphery, it looked like he put a sandwich in his pants—which I suppose was the best-case scenario. Then he walked to the exit. He said "goodnight" as he stepped out the door. That was the only noteworthy thing that happened all shift. I left my red apron in the back office and walked out the door.

When I stepped outside to take out the trash, everything was tinged with sentimentality and I started crying. I didn't feel accomplishment so much as a well-earned exhaustion. I was tired enough that I knew I'd be able to sleep—possibly the entire weekend. On Monday I would start classes and my first job that wasn't just the only thing

I could get. As I crossed 1300 East, in a delirious combination of exhaustion and desperation, I experienced one of those moments of extreme relief, as if I'd narrowly escaped something, though all I'd done was finish a job.

The light from Steve's kitchen arced into my eyes. I walked to his door.

# Driver

Nobody would tell Tamara where they found Steve's body. Tamara was Steve's girlfriend, and she had been visiting family in San Diego when Steve shot himself. She was obsessed with the details of his death. Even as early as the funeral, she talked about wanting to track down every step of his last day. This worried everyone—her mother, her coworkers, our friends from high school, me. We all wondered what she would do once she retraced his last step.

That's why no one would tell her where Steve had died. But she figured it out on her own from the highway exit number.

Shortly thereafter, she bought a gun at the pawn shop Gallenson's, the same store where Steve bought the .357 he used to shoot himself. She wanted the same model Steve bought, but the salesman talked her into a smaller, "more manageable" model. She tried to comfort me by saying that she was just curious what it was like to own a gun and that if she were ever going to kill herself, it would be some other way.

∾

After discovering the place, Tamara returned to Exit 88 often, even though her mother and her therapist told her to cut back on those visits, and even though Steve's surviving family told her that she needed to move on. She would stay there for hours, until the cold turned her ears and knuckles red.

Sometimes I went with her. She liked to bring her gun and shoot at targets. I am not sure if this was therapeutic for her, but I always came home feeling exhausted. For me, shooting did not offer the cathartic release it sometimes does in movies; I found it to be tedious, and loud. Tamara had only one set of earplugs, and I kept forgetting to buy my own, so whenever either of us pulled the trigger, a sharp vibration filled my ears. I didn't find it compelling at all, and I started to go out there more and more on my own, without her. I would drive to the train tracks and not even get out. Just sit and think for a minute and then drive off.

~

Over the course of making those drives, I grew to prefer the speed of the car to that of the bullet. My own car wasn't capable of meeting I-80's speed limit of eighty-five miles an hour, so I would use Salt Lake City's car-share program to "share" a Mazda 3. The program was meant for carless citizens to have access to automobiles for errands and tasks that required them. You picked the car up at a designated parking spot, filled it with gas before returning it, and the system would make its calculation and charge your account. But somehow it wasn't all that expensive if you drove the car all the way to Nevada—probably an unforeseen glitch in the system, as the program wasn't meant for that. I learned to drive with my mother's 1996 Chevy Astro van, and I drove two cars of my own in my twenties: a 1992 Dodge Shadow and a 1989 Chevrolet Celebrity. None of those vehicles could reach eighty miles an hour without shaking in panic, and without that signal to slow me, I would find myself hitting ninety-five in the Mazda 3 without meaning to. When the road was empty, I would regularly take it up to 105, 110, 120— as fast as I could go before I saw someone else.

That style of driving could fairly be described as "reckless," but that word also seems lacking because that's the opposite of how it felt. My brain wouldn't allow my focus to drift at that speed; the stakes were too high. I would never check my phone or consider changing the music. My concentration was so focused that I didn't think about what I had to do later that day; I didn't even think of myself as someone moving through the desert. Everything was a manageable blur of color and speed. The speed helped me lock into my own thoughts, offering temporary clarity on what had happened. It was the most focused I'd ever felt in my life, during a time when I couldn't focus on anything when sitting still.

~

Even though he had just been alive, my memories of Steve started to break down almost immediately into glimpses and associations.

I struggled to put together the plot of a single day. I'd picture him sweating in his Salt Lake City apartment with the fan on high and it would turn into his apartment in Provo with the roommate who was always home. I could picture him looking for bison on Antelope Island and then would have to focus to remember if that happened recently or when we were teenagers. I'd remember walking in a single-file line through the narrow part of the sidewalk on State Street and Steve trying to get us all to snap our fingers in unison, but was unable to place who else was there. I thought of little else that fall and was determined not to forget him and yet my mind poured it all into a muddled stream. With the number of memories set, and no new ones to create, I started to panic that I would forget Steve's voice.

~

I was enrolled in graduate school at Utah at the time of Steve's death, but after he died, I lost the patience and drive necessary to write the required papers. When someone introduced me to Adderall, I felt like I imagine some athletes might feel after discovering HGH. I don't know what it does for people who actually have a prescription, but for me, what it did was make me feel light, without any need except what was right in front of me. I wouldn't be hungry for hours until I realized I was famished. I could sit down at noon and apply Kristeva's theory of abjection to any text we happened to be reading, stay up all night, knock out a fifteen- to twenty-page paper, and hand it in the next morning. Even immediately after writing the paper, I could remember almost nothing of the writing process itself—just a hazy idea of the result. It was as if I had been offered the chance to exchange twelve hours of my life for a paper, an offer I readily accepted. And I think that's close to the exchange I made for that whole second year of graduate school. I can still remember my first year at the University of Utah vividly; I know what I ate for lunch after walking around on campus the first time; I remember being embarrassed after mispronouncing a menu item at an Italian restaurant with colleagues; the anxiety before each class; shock at how funny *Don Quixote* was; the relief of having survived. But of the second year, I remember almost nothing of campus, my classes, the books I read. I don't even remember my embarrassments.

~

The white vinyl fences on the outskirts of Salt Lake, the beaming lights of the nuclear storage facility in Tooele, the shore of Great Salt Lake, the open plains of salt lit up by the sun on the Utah-Nevada border pricking my eyes with brightness. A U-turn in Nevada with the sun on its way out and flying back over the Salt Lake desert as part of the orange-pink light in the sky.

~

During one drive, Tamara told me about a recent conversation she'd had in which her mother asked her why she kept driving out to Exit 88. "What can you possibly hope to gain from that?" she asked. The story ended with Tamara storming out of the house, but when she told me about the encounter, she told me what she wished she had said.

"It's not that I can't move on," she said. "It's that I don't want to."

If anyone had asked me why I kept speeding to Nevada and back—and nobody did, as I never told anyone about it, not even Tamara—but if they had, I probably would have undersold the frequency of the drives, reduced the digits of the speedometer. I would have said something about being in grief, and wanting a distraction from it. But thinking on it now, I was taking a cue from Tamara and clutching the recent past and present as tightly as I could. I wanted to move so fast that time would rattle and freeze, allowing Steve the space to pull over to the side of the road, breathe, wipe the sweat from his face. I wanted to think about him, still moving. I wanted the second where he could still turn around and head home. Say goodbye to his girlfriend, to me. And even if not, I didn't want to move on without him.

~

To the north of I-80, racers have used the salt flats to break speed records for years. The salt has a cooling effect on tires, and its hardness ensures that in case of a blowout the rim of the wheel will not easily dig into the ground, hurling the car. When people started racing out there, the salt was up to ten feet deep, and firm. Racers drove cars with jet engines in them and broke the sound barrier.

I have yet to read a description from anyone who's driven that fast that brings me close to what it must feel like. I enjoy the elasticity of words and am not usually thrilled to see something described as being "beyond words." However, the sensation of driving at 120 miles an hour is close to being so; 700 miles an hour seems like it might qualify. A lot of good writing is based on sensory depiction; how much can the senses even take in at such speed? Part of the thrill of moving over 100 miles an hour was that my eyes couldn't keep up. I was aware that things were happening outside my immediate vision, but all of that was dark periphery with my attention entirely devoted to the one window of light in front of me. I can remember stretches that must have lasted ten seconds, but in my memory they play out as completed plot sequences. At the same time, I don't remember feeling fidgety or anxious during the drive—a long drive at standard speeds—for more than a second. If I felt that way, I just accelerated.

In a matter of hours, I moved over land so parched and endless that I could never comprehend crossing it on foot, and right back again to where I'd started: the parking space by the downtown library. The trip didn't come with a time-zone change, but the reality that you can move so fast as to alter the way time functions was the same. I could drive to Wendover and back, completely drain every ounce of attention I was capable of giving for the day, and still be on time to sit in class as a fatigued husk with a vacant stare.

~

One bright night, Tamara drove out to Exit 88 by herself. Approaching the exit, she nodded off and her car tilted out of the speeding lane into the slow lane and then off I-80 entirely, rolling three times over the dirt and salt.

She was airlifted out. In the morning, when they determined she was physically fine, they checked Tamara into a rehab facility. She was given a DUI because of the prescription drugs in her system. They had her take classes with alcoholics and drug addicts as a condition for her release.

I showed up to meet her at the facility two days later. Tamara showed me a calendar they had her make out of construction paper. On each day she was supposed to write a reason to live. She told me that the night before the crash she'd had a dream that Steve's body was being pulled by his family on one side and by her on the other. "After all the shit he put me through, I should at least get to keep the body," she said.

After the accident, once she regained consciousness, Tamara told the paramedics that she had taken some prescription medication but she couldn't remember which pills. They told her she was very lucky. Since she had been unconscious, her body had managed to drift peacefully through the crash. Because she hadn't tensed up or reacted, she glided through.

~

The last time I saw Steve, we watched a DVD that was essentially a prolonged commercial for weapons. We were in my apartment, and Tamara was there too. I realize now that the video very possibly came from the pawn shop where he bought the weapon that killed him, though I'm not sure of that.

It was an unintentionally funny, unfathomably long video about hapless white men using old-school weapons such as spears on fake elephants. They depicted themselves as warriors on the illusion of a wide-open prairie likely filmed in a public park. They would hurl their spears at the elephants, and wouldn't bother to reshoot if the spearing didn't take. They just tried again and again until they got it.

We drank some scotch that he brought over, which was the first time I'd ever tasted it. It came in a beautiful golden bottle, but tasted like liquefied roast beef. I didn't care for it, nor has the drink grown on me over time. I had one drink, and then another. Steve was in his last semester at the U before he was to graduate with a degree in political science and I thought he'd brought the bottle to celebrate his upcoming graduation.

We stood on my balcony, which faced another balcony, but I craned my neck and looked down on the firefly grid of Salt Lake City. I saw the silhouette of Steve's brown truck parked on the street.

He'd been running every morning and was in great shape; I hadn't seen much of him that semester. I asked him if he was still thinking about joining the military, or serving a Mormon mission, two options he'd been talking about.

He said he wasn't sure, and that he'd continue working at the paint store during the spring while he figured it out.

In two more weeks, he'd be dead. I can't remember what happened beyond that point on the balcony. What is the last thing I said to him? I have no idea. Based on my custom pleasantries of departure, probably "Drive safe."

~

Night and nothing visible except the beams of my headlights and the dust particles swirling therein like snowflakes for hard to tell how long, perhaps thirty or a hundred miles until the salt flats opened up and the ground glowed. It looked as though the salt was growing.

~

Tamara's close call should have turned something in my head—taught me something about the true stakes of speeding I-80—but it didn't. Instead, I doubled-down on the same thing as her: not wanting to move on despite the wisdom that I should. A belief that I didn't have to try to make something better than what it was. Tamara was convinced that time healed wounds only at the cost of the memory's erasure. If you let time take over, Steve's face would fade and dim all too willingly, and it was better to seize it back and not let go.

I continued to drive I-80 until the week I left Utah for good, years later. To some extent, my desires changed over those years. If at first I was enacting a fantasy of time travel to bring Steve back to life, later I just wanted to be close to where he once was. I had tangled his memory with the salt of I-80, and turned Steve into the ghost of that highway. It didn't seem like something I could bottle up and take somewhere else.

Initially his death felt like a moment that would divide my life forever into the then and the now. But the now kept stretching out, with the past continuing to tincture it. Over the years, just as I'd feared would happen, there were times I could not call to mind his face. Or I'd think about him when he was seventeen and, instead of looking his age, he'd look seventeen going on some old age he'd never reach.

Every time I panicked that I had forgotten how his face looked, or how his voice sounded, I'd get in the car and drive west with the idea that it would clarify my senses and restore who he was. To some extent, it worked. That stretch around Exit 88 had a way of bringing him back to life, and I could always see him out there, even if the memories started to wash out again once I turned back toward home.

~

And that's how I spent my second-to-last night in Utah, before I moved for good: alone on I-80. My blue car was ablaze in the moonlight as I drove out to the salt flats. I was in my own car, and therefore incapable of moving as fast as usual—but I was still focused because I thought it might be the last time I saw everything. I watched with the attention of someone who might be quizzed about what he'd seen. The road was empty and the sky was blurry with stars as I flew through the salt flats for the last time. I pulled over at the rest stop where the information about the Bonneville salt flats was located and walked out onto the salt. I was the only one there. The salt creaked beneath my feet. It was lit up so bright that it looked as though the stars had shattered and fallen to the ground. I felt a romantic notion that I could taste the starlight by tasting the salt. I rolled my eyes at myself even as I considered the idea, but tasted the salt all the same. I ran on the salt for as long as I could, wanting to stay there all night, but I didn't make it. I wore myself out to the point that I thought I would fall asleep in the car if I drove home. Instead I drove to Wendover and spent the night in a casino hotel. I took a shower in my room and watched TV and slept.

In the morning, I walked out to my car in the parking lot and the sun had risen once again. Driving over the salt flats that time, I looked straight ahead, as I didn't want to take in anything new that might change the previous night's memory. But I couldn't help it; my car was too slow to maintain that kind of focus. I bobbed my head to both sides and saw the salt and then the lake and the exit where

Steve shot himself. I read the billboards and the mileage distances and saw the birds on fences along the side of the road. My mind drifted to what it was like to go faster: I remembered the light of the early morning reflecting off the glass of the downtown library where I picked up the Mazda 3. A rush of telephone poles, a church, a trailer in a field, the red symmetry of the Tooele Del Taco, the palace-y Saltair resort, the Monterey Bay in Wendover, the silo as tall as the Empire State Building.

I could remember that but couldn't replicate it in my car. I drove home and loaded my things into the trunk and backseat, and the next day drove to Texas.

# Eviction Processor

Anna left. She said she would stay at her friend Brooke's for a few nights—however long it took for me to gather my things and move out. She was the one who found the apartment, and it seemed fair that she should get to keep living there. After she left, I scraped everything that was mine out of the closet and off the bookshelves and used my feet to rake it all together into a big pile in the living room. Then I sat on the couch, and saw a pack of cigarettes on the coffee table. I wasn't sure whose they were—had Anna taken up smoking?—or maybe they'd been left by someone else.

I had a nine-month run as a smoker when I was nineteen, during which time I would smoke whenever I was stressed or anxious. (Often.) I learned to see stairs as avoidable and found the concept of speaking in groups of more than three people without smoking first to be preposterous. I quit mainly because it was too expensive, but I never considered myself a non-smoker so much as a smoker who couldn't afford to smoke. I never forgot the instant relaxation that followed the hot, bitter taste of a cigarette, and I often missed it. I stepped outside and smoked one, my first in six years.

I pressed the ash into the wooden rail, threw the butt into a red plastic cup, and went for a walk. Much of downtown Salt Lake was under construction, and I had watched the structures grow from pits in the ground to their current forms: opened-up bodies with brightly lit elevators for arteries and crane arms for limbs. At night, they were at rest, the only movement the flags at the top, waving in the breeze.

I walked all over the city, and didn't return to the apartment until after the light was turning purple. My body was tired but my chest was still tight and I knew I wouldn't be able to sleep. I brewed a pot of coffee and considered my options.

Night #3:

All of the furniture in the apartment was either Anna's straight-up, or "ours," which meant she had chosen it, and I didn't want to bother with it. So it only took me the first night to pack, but I texted Anna and told her I needed more time anyway. I felt the urge to watch all of her DVDs before I left. At first, I jumped around looking for episodes of *Seinfeld* I hadn't seen, but after that I put in a movie that opened with Ryan Reynolds in a fat suit, remembered that Anna had a lot of movies like that, and abandoned the plan. Then I contemplated replacing the *Seinfeld* discs with movies I owned, such as *Uncle Buck* and *The Buttercream Gang,* but thought that if Anna discovered the replacements in the near future she would think that I had made the switch only as part of a strategy to see her again, which would probably be true. So I left the DVDs where they belonged and started searching online for a new place to live.

Night #9:

I didn't realize how tiny the studio apartment I applied for was until I actually moved in. From the outside, the Silverado was a beautiful building, with tall, white columns, wooden doors, and large balconies. The balconies might have been the problem, as when I toured the apartment, I rushed through its insides, taking in only vague details (OK, *it exists, it has walls, it has a closet . . .*) before blitzing outside to the third-story balcony I'd seen from the street. The balcony looked even larger when standing on it, though the floor had been carpeted with some kind of coarse green material that reminded me of a miniature golf course. A stout wooden railing with chipped white paint enclosed it. The vantage point provided a clear view of the Wells Fargo building, the tallest building in Salt Lake, and I could smell sweet bread from the bakery across the street. I filled out an application and paid the deposit that day.

The message of the inside of the apartment, however, was: "You will never have anyone else over, so why trouble yourself with superfluous space?" It would be hard to fit two people in the kitchen, and even with virtually no furniture I filled up much of the floor space with boxes of books, clothing, and whatever other miscellany I'd hauled from the apartment. I fell asleep on a cot that I used to take camping.

Night #13:

As I looked at the instructions and the wooden pieces in front of me, my vision went blurry and I decided that furniture assembly was impossible without years of training. In the past, assembling a bookshelf and a bed would have been Anna's domain, as she is superhumanly proficient when it comes to construction and assembly, most likely due to her upbringing, which I always pictured consisting of nonstop, backbreaking outdoor labor with her myriad siblings except for those rare occasions when she asked pa if they could quit an hour early in order to have the last of sunlight to worship the Lord. When "we" built a coffee table from IKEA, she didn't even seem to need the instructions, as though the task required no more effort than getting dressed in the morning. I thought about calling her and saying, *Will you please come over and assemble my bookshelf and bed? This isn't a euphemism or a trick.* But then I decided, no, you have to learn to do this on your own.

After taking an hour to psych myself up, and put two drinks down, I summoned the courage to tackle the bookshelf, which seemed less complicated than the bed. It took two hours, with a break for another drink in the middle, but I built it. A version of it. The end product included a remainder of several unused pieces and one upside-down shelf. I convinced myself that the shelf was fine upside-down; it gave the bookshelf heart. I hid the unused parts. Nobody would suspect a thing, as long as they didn't look closely.

The wooden bed remained impossible to assemble and I slept on the cot again.

Night #19:

I was working when Anna texted me and told me I had forgotten some things.

Part of the stress of that summer involved employment. I had finished my degree at Utah with no job lined up. At the last minute I'd backed out of a summer job as a camp counselor in Maine. I was supposed to help the kids put together a camp newspaper. Instead, I wanted to stay in Utah and spend more time with Anna. She had just moved to Salt Lake, and we'd been having problems. But by the time the summer rolled around, I couldn't find work, and somehow the summer of unemployment had not brought us closer.

Anna was working at the restaurant a lot and I was feeling lonely and inept. Sometimes she would come home from work late, grinning and bursting with energy, ready to change her clothes and go out, a post-midnight Cinderella. I was often exhausted from a day of filling out and returning job applications, and could only go through the motions.

After weeks of applying, I took the first job offered, with a property management company. The job involved processing paperwork for evictions and then cleaning out the houses and apartment buildings once the people had left. They sent me to the jobs that didn't require any skill to do passably well: hauling trash, sledge-hammering concrete, painting, cleaning, mowing, and other tasks that follow evacuation.

I was cleaning out an office building when I read Anna's text. The business had sold tombstones, and there were still two models left out front with sample engravings featuring the last name ROBERTS. I swung by Anna's after I cleared the place out to pick up the items that I'd left behind. They ended up being those things that had been relegated to the large storage closet—mostly nerdy items of mine not fit for an adult couple to display in the open, such as comic books and a remote control R2-D2. I was glad she contacted me. I'd nearly forgotten about that R2, and I wanted to see if Anna's feelings had changed. As I hauled some boxes out to the car, she started to cry. "This is why I wanted to be out of the house when this happened," she said.

I moved close to her and asked if she was all right, if she wanted me to stay for a while and talk. She bit her fingernail and looked in the other direction. In my head, there was still a good chance that the situation would resolve, that our story would follow the plot of a sitcom—we would learn some things while apart, maybe date some people the audience would recognize as temporary because, for all their qualities, they were ill-suited to either of us as soulmates.

Anna smiled at me, but it was her service industry smile. She said, "No, not right now. Please, go."

Night #25:

I kept myself from sleep by wondering if there was someone else. When I'd asked Anna about this point blank, she'd said, "I haven't been with anyone else." When I asked if she had met someone else, she said, "This isn't about someone else. It's about us." That wasn't a no, but for some reason the prospect of someone else didn't initially threaten me. I did not believe that someone else could fit with Anna as well as she and I fit. But as I lay in my studio in the dark, the hubris of this perspective rushed me at once. What if she had been moving on for a long time?

Night #28:

Anna cons:

- Might go to church again someday if she has a kid.
- Likes spending time with her family.
- Often spends time with her family.
- Says you should spend time with her family as well.
- Actually answers if someone calls her needing a ride at 3:00 a.m., often delegating driving responsibilities.
- Wears flip-flops.
- Favors acoustic music of an emotional nature.
- Often drags you to live performances of this sort of music.
- Makes you wait until well after the show is over to congratulate the musicians on a "good show," only encouraging them.
- Not very tall.

## Night #34:

The Silverado apartment building was not a social place. No one brought me any welcome gifts, or acknowledged that I'd moved in, though I did develop a custom of nodding to some of the other tenants on the stairs. The building seemed to be full of mostly divorced and broken-up-with losers like myself, and hardly any women. I adapted to my surroundings stunningly fast: In three weeks' time I'd gone from planning new recipes with Anna to eating Michelina's microwaveable cheese manicotti and drinking inexpensive whiskey from a coffee mug, telling myself I was "too pressed for time" to cook. When my friend Joey called and asked if I wanted to go get a drink, I found myself saying, "Sure, just let me find some pants."

Walking back up the stairs afterward, I shuddered with the realization that I was home.

## Night #40:

After nearly a month in the apartment, I learned the first name of one of my neighbors: Justin. Around 9:00 p.m. he knocked on the door, and asked to borrow my phone. He was tall and bald, with tattoos on his arms and neck. His eyes were so intense that I wasn't totally sure he was asking. After hesitating, I said okay, invited him in, and slowly washed dishes in the kitchen while he had a long conversation about someone named Dallas. He concluded the phone call by saying, "You tell that motherfucker that if he doesn't back off, I will slice him up with a hacksaw, and run his skull up a fucking flag pole!"

Justin joined me in the kitchen and thanked me for letting him use my phone, though his tone was still sharp, which made him sound sarcastic. Then he launched into a story about how earlier he had left his girlfriend's apartment and he thought there were guys in the darkness watching him. He swore he heard one of them whisper his name. He assumed it was his girlfriend's ex—possibly Dallas, from the phone call. The story spiraled from there to how he did some time in prison—"some kind of 'fraud' bullshit"—and ended with Justin seeming to zone out of his own story. His eyes glossed over and he was staring out my window as he said, "Never trust a motherfucking lawyer farther than you can throw him. And that's not far, since his pockets will be full of goddamn gold." I was thinking, *So people in this apartment building do have girlfriends. . . .*

## Night #45:
Many of the residents of the Silverado smoked, and I would watch them from my own balcony with envy. The old guy on the balcony next to mine had a terrible cough—deep, throaty hurls, as though he was forcing himself to vomit. I could hear him even when I was inside, and somehow even his coughs made me want a cigarette.

## Night #46:
Singleness pros:
- Can eat food made in four minutes in the microwave.
- Don't have to hang out with Anna's family.
- Don't have to hang out with other couples.
- Able to display remote-control R2-D2 in the front room.
- There are other attractive people in the world who can now be acknowledged.

## Night #46, later:
I got drunk and called Anna. Though I knew it was a bad idea, the longer I stood alone on the balcony staring into the city, the easier it was to talk myself into it. Anna never gave me a concrete answer why we broke up—she said she "wasn't sure" about her feelings anymore and that "things" had changed—and I stayed up nights thinking about what things she meant.

It was almost midnight but that wasn't late for her; she might not even be off work yet. With one more assist from alcohol, I made the call.

She answered the phone and said, "Michael, it's late."

"Hi, Anna, it's Michael. How are you?"

"Are you all right?"

"I'm fine. I was just calling to see how you were."

"I'm fine, Michael."

"Good. That's good. So. Anna, why?"

"Oh, Michael, not right now, okay? I'm tired."

Two weeks before she broke up with me, Anna had a bad dream that woke us both up. I touched her hand and asked her what was the matter, but she turned away from me and didn't answer. That was unusual. She enjoyed recounting her dreams, often going into exhaustive, sometimes tedious detail and then inviting me to help interpret what they meant. My overused joke was that it was her subconscious telling her she wanted to make out with me. But that night, when I said, *Honey?* she just said, *Please, go back to sleep.*

<br>

## Night #59:

Walking home from work, I saw Justin on his balcony, which was on the first floor right by the building's entrance. Instead of heading in, I walked into the bakery across the street and had some coffee while I stared across the street, waiting for him to go inside.

When he finally did, I went home. But it ended up Justin had only gone inside to check his mail, and I ran into him at the mailboxes. He said, "Hey bro, we're having a party this weekend at my place."

I said, "Oh, cool."

"There will be girls there with skirts up to here"—he indicated by pressing the side of his hand on his own thigh—"so you should really come down."

<br>

## Night #62:

On the night of the party I stuffed blankets in the crack of the door and tried to stay very quiet so no one would know I was home. But the apartment was small and I couldn't think of anything to do that was silent and lightless. After a while I decided to go downstairs. I told myself I was curious about the logistics of having a party in such a tiny space.

Someone I'd never seen opened the door and asked who the fuck I was. Justin came around the corner and invited me in by putting his arm around my shoulder. "This is Mike," he said, and then he introduced me to everyone. "Mad Mark" was the one who opened the door, and Justin's girlfriend's name was Lara. She was tall and very thin. I forgot everyone else's name. There was a guy with a goatee in the kitchen, a wasted guy in a gray hoodie on the couch, and three girls in their early twenties gathered around a small TV. Two of them were playing Mario Kart. Everyone else was drinking Windex-colored drinks in plastic cups, but Justin offered me a beer.

I sat down and watched the video game. Nobody was really talking, except occasional commentary about the game (*Eat my red shell, bitch*, etc.). After about half an hour of this, one of the girls, the one not playing—and drunk beyond the ability to finish sentences—spilled herself over the couch and landed in my lap. One of the video game girls said, "Careful there, slut," and Justin said, "Damn, homie, the ladies love you!" I said, "Well, it's been fun, but I have to work in the morning." I tried to gently slide her onto the couch. "Thanks for having me over, have a great time, stay safe, I'll see you later!" I said as I sped out the door, beer in hand.

Night #65:
Who might Anna have fallen for that wasn't me? Was it Jonah, that goateed, walking *Pitchfork* review who'd worked with her on the newspaper? John, with the empathy eyebrows, whose every third sentence included a clause about being a strong feminist? Albert, who always said his blood started to run backwards when he returned to Utah County? Someone I'd never met? Maybe it wasn't someone else. I'd almost rather that it was, so that I could out-hustle whoever it was. I wasn't sure what to do if Anna had just fallen away.

Night #68:
I saw Justin on the balcony and he asked me what happened the other night. I said nothing, I was just a little hung up on someone. He said, "Ahh. Want to go bowling?"

Justin tried to write my name on the game screen as LADYKILLER but there was only space enough for LADYKIL. He called himself J

DAWG. I hadn't bowled in so long that I didn't even realize that people smoked and drank while bowling. It would have been a frustrating game without that, but I enjoyed the beer and the secondhand smoke. We played three slow games, which lasted long enough that our hair and skin and clothing absorbed the color and characteristics of cigarette smoke. Justin didn't say much, but he was as mediocre as I was, and he kept the beer coming.

### Night #71:

Smoking pros:
- Tastes good.
- Relaxing.
- Looks cool.

### Night #82:

I was good at reading Anna's face and her body. I could tell when she walked in how her day had gone. I could recognize the fiery look that meant someone had signed "Here's a tip—have a nice day!" on the receipt in lieu of an actual tip. I could sense when she was sizzling with energy, and I knew when one raised eyebrow meant suspicion, when it meant delight, and when it meant both.

Anna liked to walk barefoot, even on the road, and in the summer she would carry her shoes as she walked home from the restaurant. As soon as she got home, she liked to hurry into the bathroom to shower. Depending on how patient she looked, I would sometimes try to catch her before she got in there—while her skin smelled like lemon soap, and her hair smelled like steak—and lick her ear lobes.

I had a sweatshirt and a scarf that still smelled like she did post-work—sweaty and smoky. I threw them in the basket with the rest of my laundry. But after a second, I lifted them out, and went to the laundromat without them.

### Night #91:

After work, I rode TRAX back and forth from downtown Salt Lake

City to Sandy until it stopped running. I was writing Anna a letter. It was raining outside and not many people were out, which put me in a pensive mood. I told Anna that I loved her and wrote that I thought we would be better together if we were both less stressed out, if I could get a good job and we could move into a new apartment with hardwood floors and no cockroaches. I told her I was working on that and asked her to think about trying again.

Night #95:
Anna called me after receiving the letter. She thanked me for sending it, but said she wasn't ready to think about trying again. "I'm glad you seem to be doing okay," she said.

Night #104:
I went on a date, my first since Anna and I broke up, with a woman named Julie. I had met her years ago, before I started to date Anna, but lost touch with her after that. I still had her number and I called her from my apartment balcony one night.

I was surprised when she agreed to go out with me, and I picked her up that weekend and took her to Brewvies. Once we started drinking beer and playing pool, she didn't take long to shift from the polite formalities of catching up to lecturing and psychoanalyzing me. It was probably a debt I owed her for flaking out on her before. She let me know she remembered that and said, among other things, that "ambiguous people don't always get what they want," and that I needed to "find a better way of expressing carnal desires." She added that I looked "more filled out" than the last time she saw me.

The lecturing and insight came and went pretty fast, and left me wondering if her sole purpose in going out with me was to unload that. But she stuck around afterward, and we played pool. Though not exactly good, she was much better than I was, and the only games I won were the ones where she hit the eight ball into the wrong pocket. Brewvies played eighties music and Julie talked about the many times she had seen The Cure live.

I started to zone out of those reminiscences after a while, tuning back in to hear the sentence: "I kept waiting for a second encore, but Robert never came." I said, "Oh, really?" After a few seconds of silence, Julie said, "Want to see something?" and pulled out her phone and showed me a picture of a squirrel pulling apart its fur and revealing a Superman uniform underneath.

"Oh, you like Superman?" I said.

"Of course. He's the ultimate man," she said.

After we were done eating, I paid the check. Julie hesitated before the doorway and it took a second before it clicked that she might be waiting for me to open the door. Anna was a door opener, and I had almost forgotten that opening doors could be a part of dating. I flashed back to a memory of an acquaintance from high school, who removed the inside car handle from his Honda Civic so that when he took girls on dates they would have no choice but to wait for him to get out and open the door for them. I pictured the sunlight reflecting on the surface of the discarded door handle, a charred tongue in some empty field below the mountains. Then I opened the door for Julie.

Night #107:

I still had not purchased my own cigarettes but when Justin offered me one from his balcony my eyes lit up. I climbed up and took it. While he told a story about getting fucked over by the phone company, his eyes focused on the pigeons below just as cats watch birds on tree branches.

He snapped out of it after a while, and suddenly said, "You seem down, bro." I admitted that I kind of was. He invited me to go to the strip club during the weekend with him and his friends. I said thanks, but no thanks.

"Same girl?"

"Yep," I said.

Night #115:

I saw a blue shape a half-block ahead of me, walking down 200 South. Even from where I was, I could tell it was Anna and that she was smiling; she had a litheness to her step, and a bit of a strut. She turned right on 200 East, which was where I was stopping. I watched her glide away from there.

### Night #119:

I had to clean out the apartment of a family that had received an eviction notice for unpaid rent and had left in the middle of the night. It was amazing how much baby gear they left behind—a city of pink plastic inhabited by stuffed animals. It seemed like enough for an army of babies, but in the also-jettisoned photo of the family standing in front of the lion-head water fountain at Hogle Zoo, there was just one.

### Night #121:

My fantasies about ways to get back together with Anna started to move from future tense to past tense. Instead of thinking, "Maybe if I express what she means to me, all of it, she'll take me back, like in a movie," I started to think, "If only I had listened a little more closely when she talked about her sisters at the zoo that one day, we wouldn't have broken up."

When Anna said she wanted to break up with me, she said she often didn't know how I was feeling—she felt we were just going to be on the same plateau forever if I didn't learn to express myself better. They were cutting words, mainly because they were true, and it was one of the gifts Anna gave me that she was often okay with quiet. When I was exhausted, or just didn't want to talk, she would rub my back or let me rub hers in silence. I loved this, and she knew that, but it was hard on her. She liked to talk, but she loved to listen, too. I remembered one quiet night, in which she was rubbing my back with one hand while she placed the other hand on her temple. I asked, "What's wrong?" and she said—after a pause—"Nothing, I'm just tired."

### Night #123:

The forecast called for the weather to be freezing next week, and my job for the day was to climb up onto several rooftops and disconnect the swamp coolers so the water wouldn't turn to ice. I was supposed to unplug the swamp cooler, drain it, and wipe out the metallic gunk inside. For the ability to climb on rooftops, I actually enjoyed that job as much as any property management responsibility that didn't involve a sledgehammer. On the last roof of the day, the water in the cooler felt particularly cold, and at the shock of it I jerked my hand out too fast and cut it on the green metal sides of the cooler. I was bleeding a little, and I dabbed at the cut with the filthy rag I was using to wipe out the coolers. Waiting for the bleeding to slow caused me to pause and take in the rooftop view, which was the drip of sunset on the Wasatch Mountains. Not bad. There was a time when Anna and I would watch the sunset nearly every day, but I hadn't paid attention to it in a while. It was hard to watch it without her.

When I got home that evening, I spent most of the night applying for something else—any new position I could think of.

Night #130:
For our fifth date, Julie and I made dinner and watched a movie at her apartment. The movie was one of her favorites and involved a bunch of puppets defying the audience's expectations of what puppets do by swearing and having sex. Watching it with her was uncomfortable because she laughed almost the entire time and I could only force laughter occasionally. At the beginning of the movie I assumed this would be a good night to try expressing my carnal desires in a straightforward way, but by the time it was over I no longer felt like doing that. Instead I found myself saying, "Listen, Julie, you're wonderful, really—but I'm just not in a good place right now. . . ."

It didn't occur to me until I was driving home, but Anna would have liked that dumbass movie, and that would not have turned me off at all. The only way I could explain my actions to myself was by noting that Julie just wasn't Anna.

Night #131:
The winter smog inversion spilled over the mountains and roads and

blocked my balcony view of the Wells Fargo building. Only the bright blue lights at the top were able to shine through. Someone told me that running in that weather was like smoking a pack of cigarettes.

I was thinking about this as I walked to the 7-Eleven parking lot and stared through the windows for a long time, like a kid outside a pet store. It wasn't a Sev I'd worked at before, and it looked warm inside. I knew I shouldn't go in, but I did, and I bought my first pack of cigarettes in a long time.

I lit the first one and walked. There was no wind. Earlier in the week, it had snowed all day long, and that snow was still on the ground—but it was solid now, and when I stepped on it I didn't sink. The hard snow gave me the sense of being conveyed somewhere. I felt good. I walked all over the city. Once it was dark, I found myself outside of Anna's apartment, where I lit another cigarette. The street lights were dim and the brightest thing on the street might have been the flaming ash. It took me a few minutes before I remembered that it was creepy to stand outside your ex-girlfriend's apartment smoking a cigarette, and then I put it out. I tried to move naturally, as if I belonged there, as I turned around and walked down the hill toward my apartment.

Night #149:

I walked down to Justin's apartment and asked if he wanted to get drunk at Twilite, the bar around the corner, on me. He said, "Hell, yeah, dude, let's hit it."

By that point I was myself already so drunk I could barely stand up straight, much less focus on what Justin was saying. At the bar, he talked about the difficulty he was having finding a job, and I just nodded through everything he said, barely registering any of it. By the time we left, I had to focus to remember how to walk; but Justin guided the way and we made it back.

Night #151:

I went back to Justin's to apologize for being so drunk. I offered him one of my cigarettes and told him to just keep applying for work, something would come up. I said, "If nothing else, you can always break concrete and clean apartments with me." He said he'd think about it, but he really needed to figure out his own thing. "Fair enough," I said.

## Night #165:
Anna worked long double shifts on Thursdays and those days wore her out. She had a gift for transforming into whatever her table wanted her to be. If that meant girl straight from the little house on the prairie, something a little more flirtatious, or someone respectful of her elders, she could do all of that—but the performances exhausted her by the end of long shifts. By the time she got home on Thursdays, it was hard for her to stand. Those days I would not try to grab her and lick her ears, but would instead help her draw a hot bath.

Sometimes Anna panicked that she would never be able to wash out the smoky steakhouse smell, that it would seep into her hair permanently. On those nights I'd come in and bring her some wine. Sometimes I would wash her back as she lifted up her hair.

I was doing better; I had a job, my life was quiet, I was on my feet. But on Thursdays, it was hard not to think about the way Anna's hair dripped like willow branches over her face while I smoothed soap along her back.

I tried the bath routine myself to see if it would relax me as it had relaxed her. But the water seemed to get cold fast and then I was drinking wine in tepid water in the dark.

## Night #180:
I was offered a job; or rather, a position as a PhD student with decent funding. But it was at Texas Tech University, in Lubbock, Texas. It was a surprise offer; I had initially been wait-listed by that school, and taken that as a rejection. I had less than two weeks to decide. I didn't have any connection to the state, or much interest in moving there, and had applied in a blur along with any other job I could think of.

I walked downstairs and shared a cigarette with Justin on his balcony. I asked him what he thought I should do. He said, "Look, man, I'd just about kill for a job offer at this point. If you have a job, you should take it. Besides, there's good pussy in Texas."

Night #193:
I swirled some mouthwash and stopped by Anna's to ask if she wanted me to go to Texas, or to stay, or if she wanted to go with me.

I walked to her apartment. I brought her number up on my phone and leaned against the tree in front of the apartment building and stared at my phone screen. I was nervous, but I was running out of chances. I hit dial.

Anna answered, and, after a pause, invited me in and offered me some tea. I was relieved that she was alone. No sign of anything that wasn't hers, either. As she grabbed the cup from the cupboard, I wanted to touch her shoulder, but I didn't.

"How's work?" I said.

"You know how it is. But it's okay," she said.

The conversation continued like that, just catching up, while I thought of all the things I wanted to say. I had drafted them at home before, and this would be my last chance to share them with Anna. She was telling me about the latest news at the restaurant when everything came out at once. I said, "I miss you. I'm moving to Texas. Come with me. Or tell me to stay. Anna, sometimes I feel like my whole chemical makeup was formed to fit together with you. I don't want to move without you." She touched my hand and looked into my eyes. Hers were watering. But then she put her other hand to her temple, just above her right eye. *Oh,* that *gesture,* I thought.

By the time I stepped outside the night was almost over. The sky above the mountains was turning the color of apricots. I smoked one last cigarette on the way home and left the rest of the pack atop the mailboxes before I walked up the stairs. I didn't really want to, but I left those in Utah, too.

# Stray

QUANDARY, a problem with no solution. (*See also*: DESIRE.)
—Rebecca Lindenberg

## 7-Eleven

On Fourth Street: The convenience store where I bought "groceries" (alcohol, sodium snacks, the *Lubbock Avalanche Journal,* and apples) for my first ten days in Lubbock, Texas. *See also* **Alcoholism;** *Lubbock-Avalanche Journal.*

## Alcoholism

a) The action of alcohol upon the human system; diseased condition produced by alcohol.

b) "Not being a pussy."—Kelly. *See also* **O Bar.**

## Back Roads

On Sundays, Kelly liked to drive out of the city to look for birds. She liked all birds but studied vultures in particular. She used fence posts and trees for landmarks, and somehow knew where the birds would be. I could never find the places on my own. *See also* **Vultures.**

## "Bless Your Heart"

Rough translation: "Jesus said love everyone, but you are one sorry motherfucker."

## Car Dust

Kelly said that in the sixties, if you drove in a sandstorm from Lubbock to Abilene, the wind would blast the paint clean off your car. True or not, after my first sandstorm, I could see from my car's new brown color that the wind and dirt had made an effort. The first time this happened, I drove straight to the car wash; after it happened again, I just left it.

## Cochineal

Kelly was interested in the biology on the ground, too. If the sky was empty of vultures, we would walk around. Once, she jabbed her finger into something she called cochineal, which looked like mold growing on a cactus. She lifted her finger up to the sun and it gleamed red. She said cochineal was what people used to make red dye in the past. She wiped her red finger on her pants and continued walking.

## Conversations

Disappointing: when the girl in the blue shorts at the coffee shop sat across from me but then asked if I'd been saved.

Endless: those about high school football, those about how country music used to be more tactile, those which employ the word "rhetoric" repeatedly.

Surprising: when the girl at the O Bar introduced herself as Kelly and said she could tell I was from out of town just by the way I was watching the basketball game.

## Counterbalance

a) A weight that balances another.

b) A force or influence that offsets or checks an opposing force.

c) I said my eyes would kill for some trees or a mountain to look at, and Kelly said it's only the untrained eye that sees West Texas that way. I enjoyed hearing her talk like that and found her convincing, at least as long as she was nearby. *See also* **Mountains**.

## Dilemmas

a) Pulling up to the stoplight next to a large truck with my windows rolled down and Miley Cyrus' "Party in the USA" playing, and then having to determine whether to roll up the window, change to a station more befitting my demographic, or just leave it.

b) Realizing that Kelly's behavior was motivated at least partially by pity; wanting her to stay anyway. *See also* **Loneliness**.

## Drunk E-mails

To Joey: detailing the ways and means by which he was an asshole for not visiting yet; exaggerations of how fun the city was.

To Kelly, early on: full of attachments, pictures of birds and the sky.

To Kelly, later on: apologies and complicated explanations for not calling back earlier—but with a light, jokey tone; a distressing abundance of emoticons.

## Ear Dust
Out walking with Kelly, I couldn't hear a word she was saying because the wind and dirt were funneling into my ears.

## "Everything is Bigger in Texas"
A non-hyperbolic point of Lone Star pride. Especially accurate when considering soda sizes, highway stretches, and expanses of sky.

## Excess
The sky on the drive home from Palo Duro Canyon, so full of sunlight that my eyes started to crackle, and I finally turned most of my attention to the dashboard because my eyes just couldn't take any more in. *See also* **"Everything is Bigger in Texas"**; **Moths**; **Sun**.

## Flicker
a) A bird, related to the woodpecker, and similar in appearance, except heavier and with beady shark eyes. Their wings turn the still air into pools of sound when they take flight.

b) A pattern of light, as when sunlight filters through the trees, or light emitted by an old bulb just before burning out. *See also* **Mothlight**.

## Geese
a) They fly in bursts to the playa lakes, and fill them to the brim. They know the distance between things.

b) In the morning: loud, moving in swarming patterns far more complex than the standard V. From a distance, they look like a plague of insects.

c) At night: their stomachs draw in the moonlight and they glow in the dark.

## "A Good Christian Man"

What my twenty-year-old neighbor Tiffany told me she was trying to find, after complaining that her old boyfriend wanted to direct films instead of getting a job.

## Grackle

Unloved birds with long, wedge-shaped tails and bright yellow eyes. They appear black at a distance, but up close, in the light, their colors range from blue to green to purple, depending on the light. Kelly told me that in college, she wrote a paper explicating the grackle's ability to survive on almost anything.

## "Happiness is Lubbock in My Rearview Mirror"

Lyrics by Mac Davis, oft repeated in the region. The song tells the story of a fifteen-year-old kid yearning to bust out of town and move to the "lady in red," Hollywood. The most famous lines from the song are: "I thought happiness / was Lubbock, Texas / in my rearview mirror."

Less famously, as the song continues, after the kid does finally drive away, "stoned on the glow of the Texas moon," he finds Hollywood to be dehumanizing ("the lady in red / just wanted my last dime"). By the end of the song, he returns home ("now happiness is Lubbock, Texas / growing nearer and dearer"), and vows that he'll be buried there "in jeans."

## Haboob

a) A violent and oppressive wind which brings sand from the desert.

b) I was in my office when the haboob of 2011 hit. The sky went dark outside, but I'd lost track of time and thought it was just night. Soon after that the smoke alarms in the building went off, and I went outside. The building had misread the dust as smoke and directed us outside, where we couldn't see through the wall of dirt, which was the closest thing I'd ever seen to an avalanche, even though the dirt seemed to have nowhere to fall from.

## Horizon

The sky and sunbaked dirt stretched out further than my eyes could comprehend, and it was hard to take anything in because nothing was distinctive. The experience was kind of like looking at the ocean, except there was nothing to touch or dive into. *See also* **Excess.**

## Lightning Without Thunder

Startling charges in the purple sky unaccompanied by sound. In the quiet, the lightning seems transformed, and more like ground fire.

## Loneliness

a) While watching television, I forgot where I lived, and then remembered.

b) Kelly loved to talk on the phone, and I never had a good reason as to why I didn't want to. Still, I often wouldn't answer.

c) After fighting against it for the first few months, I eventually cocooned myself inside it, and the human interaction that seemed necessary to break the feeling started to feel less desirable than the quiet, motionless alternative. *See also* **Patience.**

## *Lubbock Avalanche-Journal*

a) The newspaper in Lubbock, named after an avalanche.

b) Front-page headlines from the first copy I bought: "Potts Wins Tech QB Starting Job," "Space Is No Issue for City Graveyards," "An Inspiration: English Teacher at Frenship Middle School Begins Her 40th Year Today," "Football Team of 1976 Succeeded Without Boasting."

## Luddite

a) One of a group of early nineteenth-century English workers who destroyed laborsaving machinery as protest.

b) One who is opposed to technological change.

c) What Kelly accused me of being, along with a "fucking hermitic weirdo," based on my reluctance to answer the phone or return texts. Luddite was probably part of it, but not the whole story, as I'm sure she knew. *See also* **Loneliness.**

## Lung Dust
Stepping inside my house after a long walk, I still felt the dust swirling in my throat.

## Mockingbird
A slender, long-tailed gray bird. It often imitates other birds, and likes to sing at night. The Audubon Society describes its call as a "harsh *chack*." Also: the Texas state bird, chosen, according to Kelly, because it will "defend its home to the death!"

## Monarch Butterfly
The state butterfly of Texas; monarchs thrive on milkweed, which is abundant in Texas. This plant is also poisonous, though not for the monarchs. This makes some monarchs poisonous for predators. However, the number of poisonous monarchs is only about 10 percent, and clever birds such as orioles have figured out ways to open monarchs up and taste-test them to see if they are poisonous, or edible.

## Moth
a) A small, soft, winged insect. Although nocturnal, they flock to the light.

b) A person who is insignificant or fragile, or one who hovers around temptation and is liable to be drawn to destruction (as a moth to a flame).

## Moths
Plague of: In the spring of 2012, moths seemed to grow out of the ground, taking over the city, swooping through the alleys like sparrows. Many of them found the lamplight in my living room. They flickered inside the lampshade like demented fairies, their bodies a collective crackle as they hurled themselves against the bulb. *See also* **"Everything is Bigger in Texas"; Excess; Mothlight.**

Shower of: When I stepped outside and closed my front door, the moths rained out of my awning, onto my head and shoulders.

## Mothlight
The shaky light, somewhat reminiscent of an old film reel, created by moths as they spin around and bounce off lamps. *See also* **Flicker**.

## Mountains
In Utah, they are stark and abundant. I never noticed how much I noticed them, until confronted with their complete absence in Lubbock.

## Ogallala Aquifer
A vast underwater aquifer, providing water for significant portions of eight different states, including the panhandle of Texas. Though vast, the aquifer is shallow. Some estimates suggest it will dry up in as few as twenty-five years.

If so, I don't see how West Texas can continue to burgeon, if it can even survive. This can lead to a feeling that one is living in a ghost town before the ghosts arrive.

## O Bar
On Thirty-Fourth Street: a smoky bar with neon and television lighting, in which Kelly said, "You'll learn to love Texas. Have another drink."

## Patience
a) In the fall, starting around September 21, millions of monarchs migrate out of their breeding range, travel down through Texas, and arrive in Mexico by November, where they cluster in the forest's fir trees, which protect them from freezing. They spend the winter there, and don't fly back for six months. They don't breed until the return trip, or they wouldn't have the motivation to make it. The next year, this new generation is able to find the same trees in Mexico.

b) What Kelly ran out of when I suggested we spend Saturday night getting drunk at the laundromat.

## Quiet
Inside my small house on the alley, aside from the wind, I often heard

only silence. No traffic, no voices; no clanking or noisy plumbing in the house. At first, this led me to drink, but after a while, I grew so comfortable in it that I would dread having to break it. *See also* **Alcoholism; Loneliness; Luddite.**

## Rain

In the gutter: When it does rain, the water surges through the streets, sometimes stalling cars. Trucks that do make it through send waves of water over the sidewalk. Sometimes the sun will be shining when this happens, and the water hooks the light.

Thirst for: After a month that never seemed to drop below ninety degrees, even at night, I could smell the rain gather in the sky as I walked home from the convenience store. Rather than speed up to beat it, I stopped and waited.

## Sky

Flashing with lightning: lively, in some ways reminiscent of hungry fish looking for food at the water's surface.

In spring: dirt and dust rise up and change the sky into a color resembling wood paneling.

Outside city limits: The distinction between background and foreground dissolves. The views go further than your eyes can follow. *See also* **Excess; Horizon.**

## Sleeplessness

a) The state of being sleepless; an inability to sleep.

b) On the hot sheets I was tempted to turn on a lamp, or even light a match, just to see how many moths were left. *See also* **Moths.**

## Snow

In West Texas, it snows lightly a couple times every year—wispy ghosts of snow dancing in the wind. The snow creates a holiday that shuts the city down.

## Sparrows

Burst of: a congregation of birds that retreats in unison when they hear the rustle of someone approaching.

## Stadium Motel

Inside: While I waited for my rented house to be made available, I stayed there. My room had wood paneling and two frames containing the same photo of white spectral trees lining a winding road. Pasted on top of one of these photos was a large sticker of Jesus Christ leading a sheep up a mountain. The kitchenette was a miniature refrigerator with a microwave on top. There were dark stains on the bathroom wall. The overhead fluorescent lights were old, and too dim to read by. *See also* **Flicker.**

Outside: People sat in front of their doors in fold-out chairs in one-hundred-degree heat and drank beer. One morning, a police officer knocked on my door looking for someone, but it wasn't me.

## Strategies

For convincing friends to visit: guilt, pictures of the sky, promise of sunshine and alcohol. *See also* **Drunk E-mails, to Joey; Sky.**

For keeping Kelly around despite never wanting to talk on the phone or commit emotionally: slightly better in-person attentiveness. But mainly: e-mails and letters full of what I perceived—especially while intoxicated—to be funny, endearing jokes. *See also* **Drunk E-mails, to Kelly.**

For staying cool in the summer: I remained in the indoor pool for as long as possible, well after being hungry, and too weak to swim a lap.

## Stray

To escape from confinement or control, to wander away from a place, one's companions, etc.

A lost creature. Examples: a pit bull with no collar crossing University Avenue. A twilight creep of cats. A solo silhouette in the field at night. Posters pasted all over the city: "Answers to Joshua. If found, please call. Reward offered." Or: "Cat found. Sick or very old."

## Students

Lubbock revolves around Texas Tech University, and 95 percent of the students there are from Texas: teenagers turned loose, on their own for the first time. In the morning their lawns are scattered with empty beer cans. Discarded T-shirts in the alley weeds. A single gold shoe resting the middle of the alley, lost by a Lubbock Cinderella.

## Sun

Afternoon: my eyes could never adjust to this much brightness.

Evening: the most pink I had ever seen in the sky. *See also* **Drunk E-mails, to Kelly; Sky.**

Motherfucking: When, driving west into the setting sun, one cannot see any of the lines on the road, the sun is so confrontational and bright.

## Sun-spill

The way the sun fills up the empty bottles in the kitchen the morning after.

## TX-349 S

A two-lane highway that leads from Lubbock to Midland. The darkness was as thick as thirty shadows and it didn't seem possible that the road would lead to a city big enough to have an airport, unless the city was Mordor.

## Vultures

a) Scavengers that feed on the dead, though they'll also eat the weak, sick, or unprotected. They soar in groups, alternately flapping and gliding, until one of them discovers something to eat, at which point the others converge on the find. When they circle, it isn't always over the dead. Sometimes they are gaining altitude for a long journey.

b) Someone who preys upon a person, the mind, etc., in the manner of a vulture.

c) Well after she was too frustrated with me to respond to my e-mails, I called Kelly, and she answered. I had been watching broad shadows stretch across the dirt in the alley, and when I walked outside, I saw dozens of large birds—some circling, some gathered in a tree. They were enormous—large enough to noticeably alter the way the sun touched my face. Kelly told me they were probably vultures. She sounded excited for a second, then remembered who I was and adopted a more measured tone. She tried to explain to me what they were doing, but I was having a hard time focusing. The shadows of the birds were pouring into my eyes.

## Wind

a) On the plains, it meets no resistance and picks up confidence. By the time it reaches the city, it snaps the state flags, scratches the windows and doors, bullies the dust into the sky.

b) Only when it was windy was there any noise in my house: the wind could rattle the walls, or lift up the awning and slam it back down as if performing a wrestling move. *See also* **Quiet.**

## Windburn

The feeling, like a rope rubbing against my ears, which I experienced when I went for a walk over the frozen gray-yellow grass in the winter.

## Windwarp

a) An effect the wind has on isolated plants all over the plains. Their shapes are changed by the wind into question marks, parentheses, and slashes. Kelly said wind-warped plants are an illustration of how West Texas is only ugly to the untrained eye.

b) Once, her car broke down and Kelly and I had to walk. We walked against the wind, both of us leaning forward as if trying to pull something, dust in our eyes and ears, struggling to make our way inside somewhere. Anywhere. *See also* **Ear Dust; Lung Dust; Patience; Stray.**

# Watcher

When I first moved out of my parents' house, I had to re-learn how to sleep. At home, quiet was guaranteed after 9:00 p.m. Even if my mom was still awake, she would just be doing crosswords in the kitchen. I found it exhilarating to lurk beneath this silence in the basement and sneak out as quietly as possible. But the silence was routine and inevitable.

In the apartment I moved into, Sharon and the band that lived upstairs kept night hours. At times, they even practiced at night, which Sharon told them was "no problem" as long as they kept the fridge in the garage stocked with beer. When the landlord paid us to tear out the carpets upstairs so he could replace them, we nailed the scraps up on the garage wall to insulate the sound, but you could still hear every word and chord of the band's passionate dedications to Jesus Christ.

When I couldn't sleep, I would watch comfort television on our thirteen-inch TV. I was watching a DVD of *Buffy*. Villains called "The Gentlemen" floated through the streets of Sunnydale. They had stolen everyone's voices. Now they wanted their hearts.

The episode didn't put me to sleep so I stepped outside and went for a walk. It was summer and the air was warm. I walked in the direction of the train station a mile west of our apartment. It was around midnight, Utah County, nobody outside. I heard the occasional car a few streets over and sometimes the punctuation of a train horn, but those sounds were for the most part sewn into the nightscape seamlessly, no more abrasive than a dim star.

When I got to the train station, I scooted down the overpass slant and started walking along the train tracks. I knew they ran through a landscape of marshland, dirt road, broken bottles, gravel, weeds, and trailers. But at night I couldn't see much of it, and the lack of sight kept me from walking too far down the tracks. I walked back and waited on the overpass, hoping for a train to approach. I waited in the quiet for about twenty minutes and was about ready to go when I heard a distant horn. I watched the light move closer and listened to the space between train horns. Even though I could never see who it was, I looked for the conductor in the front car as it got close and wondered what I would look like to someone seeing me for the first time, sitting next to a moving train after midnight.

## 2.

Blake had brown eyes with a stored energy focused in the middle, a black collapse of mostly excitement and some anger. In his LiveJournal, he wrote things like, "I recommend sex on the hills in the rain with the blue lightning reflecting off your lover's body." He was also intense in person. "Hanging out" for him often involved train hopping or dumpster diving or stealing paint. In most cases, I doubt I would have had the courage to go with him if he'd told me where he was going ahead of time. I don't know if he knew himself, until he was doing it.

I met Blake in an English class in my first semester of college. But I already knew who he was. I'd seen his band, Parallax, play before. I felt proud when he stopped me after class and asked me if I wanted to come over to his house for dinner one evening to eat vegan food. Soon thereafter, he started inviting me to parts of the state I'd never known about or imagined.

During one such drive, I asked Blake if he'd ever been to the train station by my apartment.

"Lots of times," he said. "You can see some of my work on just about all of those cars." His tag was RIOT and I had indeed seen it there.

Blake told me to park several hundred yards away because the trail that led where we were going was too narrow for a car. We walked through an unanticipated swamp to get to a dilapidated cement structure. The cement was sinking into the wet ground. There was a pond nearby and a two-story abandoned barn on its edge. It looked like the set of a horror movie. Rebar was sticking up everywhere, and there were a few caverns with water in them. Blake pointed to some skulls he had painted, and to some of his favorite murals by other artists.

He invited me to paint. I wrote my name and it looked even worse than my regular handwriting. It was bad enough that Blake didn't even have the heart to encourage me that I just needed practice. I just handed the can back to him, nodded, and walked off. I admired the art of others.

Then it was dark. My flashlight was weak and yellow, a dull push into the thick night. I was carefully watching my steps when Blake approached. As usual he acted as if everything was happening just as he had expected, and there was nothing better to do than what we were doing. I turned my light toward him and he smiled and stared brightly—his face looked scary when he smiled like that, adventure and invincibility swirling through his teeth.

"Look up," he said.

I had grown up seeing stars from my house, but those stars were dusty shards of glass in an old fire pit. When I looked up, the sky was TV-bright. The stars spilled right into the cement caverns and kept spilling, as if they were falling from a river that would keep replenishing until it froze over in the winter.

Blake was a very sincere person, and I don't think I usually saw what he wanted to show me. But that time I saw it.

### 3.

Exit 88. Bright hues all over, the train tracks blazing. The sky was a thorough, straight-up blue, so unvarying it seemed to surround me like a large plastic dome. There was a light breeze whistling along the rails. I threw rocks and pissed on the tracks while I waited for the train. When it finally arrived, I stood by my car until it was very close. Then I walked as close to the tracks as I could bear. I was near the place where Steve had shot himself, but I wasn't trying to follow him. I never intended to walk onto the tracks themselves, and if I had died it would have been by accident. I just wanted to stand close. To breathe in as much speed as I could.

4.

Anna told me where to meet her: a couple miles into the Provo trail, near Independence High School and a park rumored to be a place people met for sex after dark. But it was daytime, and that isn't why she wanted to meet there. This was in the early days. Neither of us knew how to go on dates without spending money, so we just showed each other places in Utah County that we liked.

The train bridge she wanted to show me arced right over the Provo trail, and I saw her standing up there as I approached. There was a fence between the trail and the bridge, but the post between the bridge and the chain link was tilted open like a crocodile mouth. I climbed through it.

The architecture of the bridge was a box-girder style, which created indentations on the bridge sides. There was a lot of paint up there, most of it pretty sloppy. There were large stenciled letters experimenting with texture and color. I enjoyed the amateur quality because it seemed possible, and the words were easier to read.

Anna and I talked on the bridge for a while. When we felt the rumbling she said, "Finally, let's go." She crouched in-between the indentations on the margins of the bridge. It was a tight space in there—horizontal slants of steel were placed every five feet or so for stability. "Come on," she said. I was longer than five feet, plus Anna was already in there. But she knew what she was doing, so I squeezed in, my right shoulder between her arm and her ribs. I felt the rusty metal in my hair and could smell my deodorant. Steel and Anna's body were above, below and to the side of me, but I could see the train tracks outside of our space and I scanned them for anything loose the train might knock into us when it passed.

We felt the train rumble and listened to its horn until it was passing in front of us. I closed my eyes as it approached, but it seemed to take forever for it to pass by, and I opened my eyes after a while. The movement of the train was fast and graceful for something so filthy. I looked at Anna, and her brown eyes were open too.

# Baptizing the Dead

On October 17, 2007, a Union Pacific employee called the Tooele Police Department and reported a truck vacated in the Salt Lake desert. The truck was parked next to the train tracks and had been there since just before noon. The police asked for the license plate number. The truck was registered to Stephen Krommenhoek. He was twenty-three years old and lived in Salt Lake City. They sent an officer to check it out. When the officer arrived, he found the truck windows rolled down. There were two boxes of unused ammunition and an empty water bottle on the floor.

On the other side of the train tracks, fresh shells were sprinkled on the ground. An old office chair and some Bud Light bottles were set up in the distance as targets. Past those, over a small hill and closer to the water, there was a body lying on the salty ground. The call from Union Pacific came in around 5:00 p.m. and the officer found the body around 7:30. An ambulance was called; family was notified. The body was lifted up and hauled away.

∾

After Steve died, that was about all of the story I was able to tell, despite trying to eulogize him several times. Whether writing an essay or drinking with my friends, I was never able to get far into the story without turning back or shutting it down. I couldn't handle the image of Steve lying there, face down in the salt, with the distant I-80 traffic zooming past him. Every time I tried to tell the story, I just wanted to put him back in his truck, and bring him home.

Tamara, Steve's girlfriend, responded to his death in the opposite way. She couldn't *not* talk about it. In any context, to anyone. She couldn't go a day without bringing Steve up. It didn't stop her if her audience didn't know Steve, nor would she pause for those who knew him well. In my case, she seemed to like it when I just listened without saying anything, and we started to spend a lot of time together—much more than we ever had when Steve was alive.

In some of Tamara's versions she recounted what Steve must have done that day. Other times she blamed herself for being in San Diego when it happened. And sometimes she presented the story as a small blip of something much bigger—something as long as eternity. When Tamara talked about Steve's death as part of the eternal scheme of things, she started by telling me that he prayed every night. That was something I didn't know about him.

Sometimes Tamara took comfort in her Mormon faith. Other times she said that the pressures of being a righteous priesthood holder drove Steve to the pawn shop, and the inability of the Mormon church to find a place for nuance put the .357 Magnum in his hand.

Still, Tamara was occasionally able to calm herself down when thinking about two things: first, that she'd be able to see Steve again after she died, and second, that at some point while reclining in the passenger seat of his truck before he walked off and shot himself, Steve was comforted, and felt some kind of peace in the desert before he left.

That was one reason why I couldn't tell Steve's story as freely or as well. When I imagined him leaning the seat of his truck back as far as it would go, I saw him staring at the brown metallic ceiling, and seeing only that.

～

I did not know Steve's parents well. When we would go to the house he grew up in, it was always clean and quiet. His mom and stepdad lived there; his parents were divorced. All Steve had to say about his dad was that he was a "Dutch son of a bitch." Besides that, I knew he gave Steve his last name, Krommenhoek, as well as the genes contributing to characteristics seen nowhere in his mother: relative height, lighter skin. His mom's side of the family had moved to Utah from Mexico. As far as I'm aware, she never talked much about that journey, though Steve did tell me that sometime shortly after their arrival they were greeted with burning crosses on their front lawn. Steve was the youngest of three kids.

Steve was about six feet tall, with a body that had adapted

itself to carrying around multiple cans of paint every day for years. Bulky shoulders, balanced steps. He worked for Sherwin-Williams, delivering paint to work sites in his pickup truck. He routinely carried four open cans in each hand up flights of stairs without resting or spilling a drop.

I helped him one day when I was bored and we had plans that couldn't start until he was done. I spilled paint twice, which seemed to just confuse him. Those deliberate steps were just an inseparable part of his overall movement. I asked him to explain how he did it and I might as well have asked him to explain how his legs walked.

He had a scar on his left arm just below the elbow, more like two scars earned at the same time, parallel horizontal gashes lying side-by-side like a railroad track. He got those as a kid when he was testing the new pavement at Daylight Donuts on his skateboard. He lost control going down the slope and flew arms-first through the window. He couldn't pull them back, so he just had to wait there, bleeding onto the linoleum floor on the other side, until someone noticed. Daylight Donuts is on State Street, so it didn't take long, and he was all right. He was on the news that night.

∾

For the most part, when I stopped attending church, I would admit to only the benefits of that choice. But I was lonely. I lived in a community that was 85 percent Mormon. Mormons don't have a Catholic-style hell, and, in fact, the lower kingdoms in Mormon heaven seem pretty pleasant comparatively, except for the loneliness. If you mess up your life and end up there, you will miss the Savior's warm glow. You will miss your family.

I once had a seminary teacher contrast our time on this planet with eternity by tying a string up to the blackboard and extending it out of our classroom and through the entire building. He told us to imagine that it stretched all the way over Mount Timpanogos to the east. Then he placed a clothespin on the string and told us the clothespin represented the time of our mortal existence. The string, the one we were imagining stretched over the mountains, represented the eternity that was up next. "What in this life is worth giving all

166

that up?" he asked. "A beer?" It's not the most robust theology, but that string stretching over Mount Timpanogos was the image that came back to me for years afterward, every time I did something new that wasn't allowed in Mormonism.

～

About four months before he died, I asked Steve why he was still going to church. My tone was jesting, but I was genuinely curious. He was an adult, he lived far enough away from his family, and he was an unmarried non-virgin who liked to drink. Yet he still went sometimes, skipping out only when he was too hung over or had too much work to do. The topic of religion came up because Steve was drunk and admitted that he was still thinking about serving a Mormon mission even though he was twenty-three and hadn't gone at nineteen, the standard age for male missionaries at the time.

For the most part it wasn't a profound conversation. Before I asked him why he went to church I became visibly angry because Steve disagreed with my assertion that Wonder Woman would beat the Angel Moroni, the gold angel on the top of most LDS temples, in a fight. *What's he going to do, Steve, trumpet her to death? Is that what you think?*

He shrugged off my question about going to church for a while, but eventually said that he just wanted to be a good Christian. I remember his answer because it didn't sound sarcastic. We seldom spoke earnestly on the subject of religion, and I didn't know what to say. I just took another drink from my glass.

～

After I graduated from high school, I did not know what to do with myself. As a result, I mostly followed others. I pinballed to the East Coast and back; piggybacked on the work others had done to locate jobs and apartments. At first, I told people that I was kind of Mormon, but later I avoided bringing it up at all, so I wouldn't have to get into whatever that meant. I didn't even like to say that I was from Utah, to avoid the inevitable follow-up question, and then the inevitable follow-up questions after that. I didn't realize it at the time, but I wanted to erase that part of me, and I volunteered the information that I'd grown up Mormon only if I needed to lower expectations.

I still revert to that tactic every so often, but while I never did regain my faith, I did reclaim some part of my people and my background, and Steve was a big part of that. We moved to Salt Lake City around the same time. Neither of us knew many people there, and we spent a lot of time together.

We both had Thursdays off, and usually in the afternoon he would pick me up in his truck, and we would figure out something to do. He wouldn't actually enter the neighborhood in which I lived, the Avenues, because he said it was the only protest he could think of for me since I'd moved from Utah County into a neighborhood where the dogs don't bark, where yoga studios outnumber churches, and where the cowboy hat was worn, if at all, only as an ironic accessory.

So I'd walk down three streets and meet him in the parking lot of the bagel shop on the Avenues threshold. Steve would wait for me there in the back of his rusty brown pickup truck, often with a cigarette in his smiling mouth.

I even went to church with him a couple of times because I had nothing better to do and wondered how I would experience it as an adult. And though I never redeveloped a testimony, that's when I stopped denying that I'd ever been there. I re-familiarized myself with the language and the idea of being perpetually open to revelation. And while my practice of the religion never went much deeper than telling annoying people at parties that their beliefs really seemed in line with Mormonism and asking them if they'd like me to send the missionaries by, usually clearing some couch space, I started to remember what it was like to see everything through a spiritual prism. To see God's work in every particle.

≈

Steve couldn't quite get it right. He was Mormon, unambiguously, but he drank, and he got angry when he did. He punched a hole in his apartment wall when his neighbor refused to turn down the music on a weeknight, after Steve had "asked politely." He went to church, but had a hard time not feeling resentment for the other people in his ward who had so much money, and were proud of it. Tamara was pushing marriage, and I think he wanted to marry her, too, but he wanted to marry her as someone better than he currently was. He felt the same way about serving a mission. A big part of him really did still want to do it, while another part told him he was in no way worthy or prepared for such a thing.

∾

When I got the phone call from Jeff that Steve's truck had been found, but Steve was still missing, I pictured him jumping off a bridge and being carried downstream by water. I didn't know why, and I tried to shake the image right away. The call came at night, around six thirty, about an hour before the emergency personnel would have been lifting Steve's bulky body out of the salt and the sand. I was on Legacy Bridge above the University of Utah pacing nervously and making final edits to a piece that I was planning to perform at a reading that night.

After the phone call, I froze on the bridge for a while, but the reading was in half an hour. I couldn't slip out on such short notice, I told myself. I went to the reading, read, and even lingered afterward for a few minutes.

For months afterward I had a lot of conversations about how there was nothing anyone could have done, but I also knew that what was meant by that was there was nothing anyone could do now. I also knew that I should have done better for my friend who shot himself in the desert than to just continue through my night, trying to get laughs at a reading. I should have been out combing the salt for his body, or at least waiting with his mom in the cold October night air while they carried him in.

∾

The funeral was a few days later in Utah County. It was a Mormon funeral, and from my perspective, it was ghastly. Steve's brother Sid spoke, which was appropriate and good—he talked about how Steve always stood with the underdog. But after that it was just stock bishops and distant family members, no one who knew Steve especially well. They tried to turn his story into a parable about how

169

the Lord works in mysterious ways.

After the funeral, Tamara and I left, still in our church clothes, to see the place for the first time. We didn't have much to go on, but Tamara had overheard the exit number—88. So we left the chapel and drove on I-80 West looking for it. I-80 changed from urban Salt Lake City to wide open nothing pretty fast, and twenty minutes from the freeway entrance there was only space, divided every so often by billboards for the Nevada gambling town Wendover that read, *The Streamline of fun is minutes away!* After about forty minutes of driving, we saw our exit and took it. We hoped we could just figure it out from there.

The frontage road wasn't paved and Tamara apologized for the shakiness of the ride. She wound past the makeshift train station, which consisted of a few trailers, a generator, and some metal Union Pacific signs, then pulled in front of a locked gate that prevented cars from crossing the train tracks. We parked the car and hopped the gate.

We could see the tracks of a heavy vehicle in the mud and we followed them, guessing that they might have been left by whatever had to drive out and pick up Steve's body. It was cold and the ruts made by the tires were frozen solid.

I picked up empty boxes of ammunition, checked the expiration dates on some bottles of Bud Light. The bottles were months old. Clearly people besides Steve came out there to shoot—there were way too many shells, targets, and bullet holes for any one person, even those Utahns most devoted to guns.

Except for the salt plant to the west, there were few shadows. Shotgun shells were part of the water were part of the sand were part of the mud were part of the railroad were part of the sound and the atmosphere and the cold wind in our ears. We were able to find the exact spot where Steve died because some of his blood was still on the ground. It was surrounded by three small flags and by this time looked like the remnants of a fire. Tamara broke down when she saw that and fell to her knees. I put my hand on her back for a little while, but when that didn't seem to help, I left her alone and walked to the shore of Great Salt Lake.

It was quiet. You could still see I-80 from where we were, and if the drivers had pulled over and known where to look, they could have seen Steve shooting his gun out there. But the distant traffic was just a hum. When I looked out onto the lake, the last thing Steve saw, I held my breath and listened to the slow rhythm of the thick water's movement. It was calming. It felt as though if I just stood there, waited, and watched, the water would creep up to my waist and then up to my mouth before I even realized it.

∾

When I was twelve, I went with a van full of kids my age to the Mount Timpanogos temple to do baptisms for the dead. Mormons perform these baptisms in the temple for those who have died without the opportunity to learn the gospel. The idea is that with baptism by proxy, the soul waiting in spirit prison will then have the choice to accept the truth, and move into the kingdom of heaven. Even if one accepts the gospel as a spirit after death, it's no good without a baptism. Spirits can't be baptized. It has to be flesh and blood.

Once you're twelve, if you can get a recommendation from the bishop, you are old enough to be baptized for the dead—really your only ticket into the temple at that age except for temple dedications.

It was raining when we gathered in the church parking lot. Steve was there. It was the first time stepping inside the temple for most of us, and everyone was quiet while we rode in the van. When we arrived at the temple, all we could hear was the light rain touching the pavement. Inside, we changed from our normal church clothes into the all-white temple clothing. In the changing room, some of the deacons broke the silence to express the hope that they would be baptized for someone famous.

After changing, I sat by Steve on a bench. He hadn't said a word the whole time and wouldn't until we were back home.

When everyone was ready, we walked into the room where the baptisms were to take place. The baptismal font was held up by twelve marble oxen pillars. Marble steps led into the font from both sides.

Mormon kids get baptized for their own souls at age eight, and the only images I remember from my own baptism were the handlebars of my bike as I rode it around the neighborhood beforehand, glimpses of yellow light in the dressing room, and the blue-leather set of scriptures that was given to me with my name embossed on the cover afterward. Other than that, I just remember feeling nervous all day. I was afraid that I would mess up, that a toe would lift out of the water and I'd have to do it again. And I was afraid to be washing my sins away now, knowing I wouldn't get to do it again.

In the temple I was near the back of the line of people to be baptized, right behind Steve. I was nervous and didn't pay attention to the first few who went, as I was again trying to focus on not screwing up. But I watched closely when Steve went right before me, mainly because I wanted to see if I could learn anything. Brother Anderson closed his eyes and bowed his head. He extended his left arm, and Steve rested his arms on top of it. Then Brother Anderson raised his right arm. *Having been commissioned of Jesus Christ, I baptize you in the name of the Father, and of the Son, and of the Holy Ghost. Amen.* Brother Anderson held Steve's wrists and guided him under the water, then lifted his body back up. The water dripped, poured, off his garments and hair. For some reason that image helped put me at ease. When I was baptized for myself, I was afraid, but when I stepped into the water this time, I was calm. I felt ready.

I know that ritual is creepy and audacious to a lot of people, but that image of water falling from Steve's eyes and hair as he crossed to the other side of the baptismal font made all my years of church and seminary and broom hockey and all the other Mormon activities worth it. When I think about that, I almost become religious again, or at the very least feel as though the things we make true are true.

~

Once, in a medication-addled dream, Tamara saw Steve. He was standing on the water of Great Salt Lake in front of the place where he shot himself. She told me his eyes were steady, but his head was dark, as though he were underwater, not above it. When he looked at her, she saw light behind his teeth.

I would like more than anything to see my friend moving again too. I want to hold on to everything I love that's vanished. Sometimes I let myself hope I will one day. But I don't ever truly believe it. At best, maybe I can try to lift him back up for a while, even if only for my sake.

~

It was autumn in Salt Lake City. The light was orange and so were the trees. The magpies that always hung around outside Steve's apartment in the morning were turning purple in the sunlight. Steve left his apartment and walked to the Gandolfo's on the hill where he bought and ate a sandwich. Afterward he went next door to Wells Fargo and emptied his checking account. He once worked at that bank, in between Sherwin-Williams gigs, and he recognized a few of the tellers and asked how they were doing. They were all right. Same old.

He got in his truck and drove downhill toward the city. He got a speeding ticket on the hill for going thirty-seven in a twenty-five miles an hour zone, an easy thing to do in a truck on that slope. After the cop drove off, he continued down the hill and stopped at Gallenson's Pawn Shop on Second South. He had been there before and knew what he wanted. He asked for the .357 Magnum he'd had set aside. It cost $750 dollars, the most he'd spent on any one thing since he bought his truck years ago. He put the gun in the glove box and headed toward I-80.

On I-80 Steve saw a car pulled over to the shoulder. The driver was staring at a flat tire with his head cocked to the side. Steve thought about asking if he needed help, but didn't commit to stopping until he was a half mile down the road. From there he would have to put the truck in reverse, and he wondered if it would alarm rather than relieve the owner of the flat tire to see a rusty pickup truck driving backwards, throwing a cloud of dust into him. He might be able to pull off two illegal U-turns. He believed in the principle that a person couldn't get two tickets in the same day. But the ground in between I-80 East and I-80 West was rocky, and fenced off in some places. His mom would have told him to help change that tire but he was too far away now.

So he drove. He felt something hot in his temples and he tried to cool down by rolling down the window and driving fast. He thought for a second of following the road all the way to Wendover and gambling the rest of his money, but he wasn't in the mood for crowds.

He took Exit 88 off the freeway. It led to the frontage road and the train tracks. Steve didn't park straightaway, but drove his truck around the dirt trails the same way he used to drive in circles around Utah Lake, with dust drifting on both sides of him. The water of Great Salt Lake was thicker, and it didn't have Utah Lake's carp that jump violently above the surface as though trying to attack seagulls. But the area had most of what Utah had to offer—sand, water, wind, trains, space, and quiet.

He parked his truck in front of the train tracks and rolled down the window, leaned his shoulder on the side of the door. The radio sounds went out into the air and he grew tired of them and shut off the engine. It was pure quiet. He looked out at the salty desert. He would graduate from school in two months. It was a time to develop new routines, to plot new trajectories.

He imagined taking a trip with Tamara into the mountains. They had once taken a directionless vacation together and wound up staying in a guest house in central Idaho. It was the best vacation he had ever taken, and sometimes he fantasized about returning to Idaho forever, owning some land, having a job where he could use his hands. He knew that vision was over-romanticized but he liked the idea of having miles of open space and something to do every day.

Thinking about Tamara and those possibilities, he considered turning around and finding her, but he was tired. He stepped out of the truck and walked to the gate in front of the train tracks. He waited there for a while until he heard a train approaching, then he lifted himself onto the gate to watch it. He lit a cigarette and stared straight ahead as the train approached and then sped away.

After the train passed, it was quiet again. Steve walked back to the truck, took out his .357 Magnum and the ammunition from under the seat. He crossed the train tracks and fired his gun at an office chair surrounded by beer bottles standing up like flag poles.

He had purchased a lot of extra ammunition and planned to use it all but he was surprised by how tiresome shooting became, especially because his aim was off and he missed most of the targets. There was something tedious about missing a target and seeing dirt rise from the ground and then slowly drift back down. He saw the half-light orange sun in the distance and knew that the sky would soon turn ashy and then dark.

He climbed back into the passenger side of the truck, leaned the seat back as far as it would go, and stared up at the brown, metallic ceiling for a long time.

In Tamara's version, that's where Steve felt peace. I hope she's right. I don't know what went through his mind before he stepped out of the truck. But he did step outside. He took a bottle of water out of the truck bed and drank it. He dropped the empty bottle on the floor of his truck with the unused boxes of ammunition. He closed the door, took a deep breath and walked in the direction of the water.

# Acknowledgments

Earlier versions of these chapters first appeared in *Bellingham Review*, *Pilgrimage*, *Alligator Juniper*, *CutBank*, *Cobalt Review*, *Georgetown Review*, *NANO Fiction*, *West Texas Review*, *Unbound Press: An Anthology of Short-Shorts*, *Rappahanock Review*, *Terrain.org*, and *RiverSedge*. A sincere thank you to the editors of those publications.

This book took a long time for me to write, and I've been helped by so many people that it would be impossible to list them all. But I would like to thank my colleagues and friends from the University of Utah and Texas Tech University for helping me with early drafts. I'm also grateful for writing residencies from the Vermont Studio Center and the Edward Albee Foundation. For help in the manuscript's later stages, thanks to Christine Marshall, Jonathan Heinen, and Ladies Prose Group.

Thanks to Sarah Bauhan, Mary Ann Faughnan, Henry James, and the entire team at Bauhan Publishing for making this possible. Thanks to Thao Thai for the perfect cover design.

I would never have tried writing a word without my first and best teacher, Karin Anderson.

Most of all, thanks to the GOAT, Kathleen Blackburn. For everything.

## The Monadnock Essay Collection Prize

This contest was started in 2017 to encourage essayists to gather their work into book form. The prize is awarded for a book-length collection (120-160 pages or 50,000-60,000 words) of nonfiction essays. The essays can take any form: personal essays, memoir in essay form, narrative nonfiction, commentary, travel, historical account etc.

For more guidelines please go to our web page or to Submittable: www.bauhanpublishing.com/the-monadnock-essay-collection-prize/ or to www.bauhanpublishing.submittable.com/submit

NEIL MATHISON was winner of the first **Monadnock Essay Collection Prize**, in 2016. In 2017 his collection *Volcano, an A to Z* was published. He is an essayist and short story writer who lives in Seattle, Washington, Friday Harbor, Washington, and Ketchum, Idaho. A US Naval Academy graduate, Mathison has been a naval officer, a nuclear engineer, an expatriate businessman living in Hong Kong, a corporate vice president, and a stay-at-home-dad. His work has appeared in *The Ontario Review*, *Kenyon Review*, and *Georgia Review*, among many others.

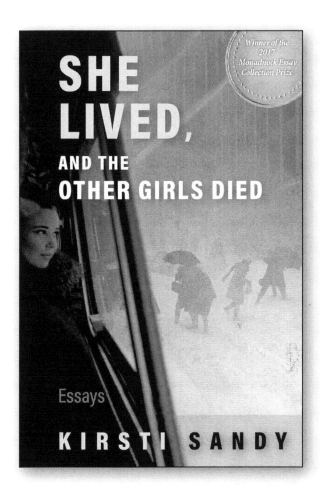

KIRSTI SANDY was winner of the second Monadnock Essay Collection Prize, in 2017. In 2018 her collection *She Lived, and the Other Girls Died* was published. Sandy teaches creative nonfiction, memoir, and narrative theory at Keene State College. Her work has appeared in *The Boiler*, *Under the Gum Tree*, *Natural Bridge*, and *Split Lip*, among other journals, and she was the recipient of the Northern New England Review's 2017 Raven Prize for Creative Nonfiction. She lives on a hill overlooking the mountains of Vermont with her husband, daughter, and, at last count, twenty-six pets (her daughter counts each fish individually).